Bloody Summer

NICK SWEET

Dedicated to my father, Ronald Joseph Sweet, in loving memory

TERCIO DE VARAS

The matador *offered the cape and the bull stood stock-still. Then it charged, and it looked for a moment as though the bull would gore the matador. But when it hooked upwards with its horns, it found only the cape and empty air.*

Chapter 1

July 1998, Seville

The victim had been forced over the back of an armchair and tied. There was a lot of dried blood, as well as some excrement, on the backs of his legs. The legs themselves were white and spindly, practically hairless. Thick green varicose veins snaked their way down the backs of the thighs and calves. They were the legs of a very old man. The handle of a kitchen knife protruded from between the flat, white buttocks.

Inspector Jefe Velázquez got down on his haunches to look at the victim's face, the old man's cheek resting against the worn leather upholstery of the chair. The gag would have prevented his screams from being heard, but the eyes told of unspeakable terror and agony. Velázquez didn't recognize him.

He began to inspect the head, bald save for a tonsure of grey hair and patched with age spots and moles. The wispy hair at the back of the head had some blood in it. Now dry, it had trickled down the victim's neck and stained his dog collar.

Who'd want to kill a priest? Velázquez wondered. And why? Could this be politically motivated? Certainly there were people out there who blamed the clergy for just about every disaster that had ever been visited on the country, right from the days of Torquemada down to the latest child abuse scandal.

The stench of the victim's excrement had begun to attract the attention of a number of flies. He laid the back of his hand against the victim's cheek. Still warm. Can't have been killed very long ago, he concluded. A matter of an hour or two at most. Maybe less. Although he'd need the Médico Forense to confirm that. Velázquez took a pair of nitrile gloves from his breast pocket and put them on, then gently parted the bloodied hair.

The scalp was badly bruised, indicating that the murderer came at him from behind with a hard solid object. He must have hit him first, then used the knife afterwards.

There was always a chance the killer had left whatever he hit the victim with at the crime scene. Velázquez searched the room, just in case, but failed to find what he was looking for.

Next he went through the victim's pockets. He found a wallet and inspected its contents.

He found some paper money–twenty-five thousand *pesetas* in total –and a number of plastic cards. He took the cards out and looked at them. Three credit cards, a library card, the deceased's *carné de identidad*, and another card bearing the name of the church where the deceased had served.

He had just finished making a note of the deceased's name, the number on his ID card and the name of the church, when he heard the familiar voice of Subinspector José Gajardo, with its heavy Sevillan accent. Gajardo was talking to the uniform standing guard out in the hallway. Moments later he came into the room. 'Got here as soon as I could, boss,' the Subinspector said, his eyes flashing with excitement.

Looking at his number two in his light-blue suit, Velázquez said, 'New threads, José?'

'They've got a sale on over at the Corte Ingles, so I thought I'd treat myself.' Gajardo smiled and held his arms out to show off his new acquisition. 'What do you reckon?'

The pale grey number fitted the Subinspector's lean athletic frame to a tee. 'Nice,' Velázquez had to admit, feeling underdressed in his black denims and polo shirt. He dismissed the notion from his mind. This was a fucking crime scene, not a fashion show.

'There was a big accident,' Gajardo said. 'I came the long way round, to avoid getting stuck in traffic. Anyway, I don't s'pose I've missed much?'

'The victim certainly isn't going anywhere fast, if that's what you mean.'

'So where's the body?'

'In here.' Velázquez pointed, and stood aside to allow Gajardo to pass through the doorway. He wondered once more about the significance of the victim's being a priest. Men of the cloth were supposed to be caring, paternal figures, weren't they? Wasn't that why everyone called them 'Father'? Maybe, but the clergy had done a lot of bad stuff down through the years, and there were people who remembered.

When Gajardo saw the victim, his thick black brows rose and squirmed like caterpillars with money trouble. The word '*Joder*' escaped from the Subinspector's lips in a quiet, involuntary lament that filled the room for an instant like a short prayer. Then he noticed the dog collar. 'Have we got an ID, boss?'

The Inspector Jefe nodded and said, 'Father Pedro Moro. He served at the church of Jesús del Gran Poder.' It was over on the Plaza de San Lorenzo, just a stone's throw from the Inspector Jefe's flat, in the Old Quarter or *casco antiguo*.

'I know it.' It would be difficult to find a grown Sevillano who didn't. 'Want me to call the Científicos, boss?'

'They're already on their way, and so's the judge.'

Velázquez glanced round the room, which had served as a study. There was a desk over in the far corner, a worn leather sofa matched the easy chair the victim had been strapped to, and shelves crammed with books ran along one wall. Ecclesiastical volumes, bound in Moroccan leather. The rest of the wall space was covered with religious paintings and icons. He recognized one of the oils, a Zurbarán copy: a slight figure standing before a number of monks and a woman who looked like a nun.

He parted the slats of the venetian blind and peered down from the first-floor window on Calle Viriato, a narrow street in the heart of Seville. Two men were going past on the pavement, both dressed in smart business suits. They walked fast, one waving his hands as he talked. Velázquez wondered what those men would think if they saw the murder scene. He had no doubt that they would be shocked, horrified. Things like that just didn't happen here. Not in Seville. Or if they happened at all, then it would be out in the notorious Tres Mil Viviendas, where a good proportion of the city's gypsy population lived. But not in elegant apartment blocks on Calle Viriato, in the heart of well-to-do Campana.

Velázquez took a look round the rest of the flat. The bedroom at the back overlooked a shaded inner courtyard dominated by a fountain, offering respite from the heat. It could almost be the sixteen hundreds, Velázquez thought.

An inspection of the kitchen and small bathroom gave no indication of a violent struggle, or anything that might suggest an intruder's presence. Neither did the lock on the front door show any signs of forced entry.

Velázquez picked up the telephone, got up the last number that had been called and made a note of it. He took out his mobile, called the number, and stood looking at the blood on the Turkish rug as he listened to the ringtone. Somebody picked up, and Velázquez said, '*Hola*, I'm Father Pedro.' A woman's voice that was to sex what Verdi was to opera told him he was through to the Express Escort Agency. 'I called a while ago,' he said. 'I'm on Calle Viriato.'

'*Si,* we sent a lad round to you over an hour ago. Hasn't he arrived yet?'

'No…what's the name of the lad again?'

'My colleague's just finished her shift, but she should've left a note. Let me have a look.' The line went quiet for a moment, before the woman said, 'Ramón… but it says here you asked for him specifically.'

'Yes, that's right. His name escaped me for a moment.'

'He's not normally late.'

'Where's your office?'

'On Menendez Pelayo. But he's not here, so there's no point in your coming–'

'Give me the number anyway, just in case he doesn't show. I might call over and take a look through your catalogue, if you have one.'

The woman told him and Velázquez wrote it down. 'He's probably got caught in traffic,' she said. 'Why don't you give it twenty minutes or so, then call again if he hasn't arrived?'

'Okay.'

The woman hung up, and Velázquez stood there for a moment looking into the helix of the receiver like he expected a genie to pop out of it. Then he replaced the handset, his mind working fast.

Gajardo said, 'What was that all about, boss?'

Velázquez ran a hand through his wavy black hair, which was flecked with grey at the sides. 'Seems the priest called an escort

4

agency. He made a specific request for a lad called Ramón and they sent him over here.'

'Looks a bit old to be getting up to that sort of thing.'

Velázquez took out his notepad and flipped through the pages, then stopped when he'd found what he was looking for. 'He was a couple of months shy of his seventy-eighth birthday.'

'How'd you know that?'

'I made a note of his birthday. It's on his identity card, which was in his pocket.'

Gajardo frowned. 'So this Ramón could be here any moment, then?'

'Could be…unless he's already come and gone.'

'You mean it could've been him that – '

'Let's not jump to any rash conclusions, José.'

Moments later the Médico Forense, Juan Gómez, came through the door. A stocky man in his early sixties, he was dressed in a linen jacket, jeans and a sky-blue shirt that he wore open at the collar. He and Velázquez were old friends, and they acknowledged each other, before Gómez set his briefcase down. Then he saw the body. '*Joder*. What a mess.'

The Médico Forense slipped on a pair of nitrile gloves, then parted the victim's bloodstained buttocks and gently eased out the butcher's knife. A jet of blood spurted out, sullying his jeans.

He dropped the knife into a plastic bag, which he then labelled. 'The científicos will want to look at this,' he said, and set the knife down, in its bag, on a nearby table.

Turning his attention to the victim once more, Gómez parted the old priest's lank buttocks again and took a look at the damage that had been done to the anus. 'That's interesting,' he said.

'What is?' Velázquez wanted to know.

Gómez straightened up. 'Seems like he was shot up the anus first.'

In his preliminary examination of the property, Velázquez had found no sign of a gun.

Gómez opened his briefcase, produced a thermometer and slipped it under the victim's tongue.

Velázquez said, 'The body's still warm, I noticed.'

Gómez held the thermometer up to the light. 'You're right, Luis…the time of death couldn't've been very much more than an hour ago, if that.'

Velázquez glanced at his watch: it was now 20:06. And he'd arrived on the scene himself some twenty minutes ago. But who was it that reported the murder? Perhaps it had been the killer that called it in.

But why would a person kill someone and then call the police to tell them what they'd done?

Just then, the short and obese form of the Instructing Judge, Cristobal Montero, entered the room, bringing with him a whiff of Havana cigars and the aura of assurance you would expect from somebody in his position. Judge Cristobal Montero's lips pursed, as if about to bestow a kiss, when he saw the victim. He turned to Velázquez. 'What have you got, Inspector Jefe?'

'The victim was hit from behind, tied up and shot up the anus, Judge. Then the killer followed up with a kitchen knife.'

Montero nodded, then ran a hand over his greying beard. 'Perhaps he was worried the bullet hadn't done the job, and wanted to ram the point home, as it were.'

Velázquez looked at the Médico Forense and said, 'I'll need you to get the bullet out a.s.a.p., Juan, for the Científicos.'

Gómez nodded. 'Don't worry, Luis, I'll make this one my first priority.'

'Have you got any leads, Inspector?' Judge Montero wanted to know.

Velázquez quickly brought him up to speed regarding the escort.

'I think I'll call round there now,' the Inspector Jefe said, 'and see if I can find out any more.'

'Shall I come?' asked Subinspector, Gajardo.

'No, you stay here, José, in case this Ramón character shows.'

'What shall I do if he does?'

'If you want my advice,' Velázquez said, 'don't turn your back on the guy.'

Velázquez climbed into the Seat Ibiza he'd been driving ever since his old Alfa Romeo was stolen and set off through the narrow streets. The pavements and cafes were packed with people as he drove through the centre. He headed down Resolana right to the end, then skirted the ancient city walls, passed the building that housed the Parlamento de Andalucía and pulled up outside a rank of shops. He climbed out of his car and entered through a doorway that was squeezed in between a boutique and a green grocer's. He ran up the stairs to the first floor, and rang the buzzer by the side of a door that had THE EXPRESS ESCORT AGENCY written on it in bold print. '*Hola?*'

'I'm looking for a little company,' Velázquez said, and the girl buzzed him in.

The reception area was shiny-new, with varnished wooden boards and white-painted walls adorned with prints. Velázquez's eye came to rest on one of them. Done in black against a bare white surface, it was a painting of a bull charging at a *matador's* cape. A girl was sitting behind the reception desk, all cello curves and scarlet lipstick. 'Good afternoon, *señor*. Can I help you?' She flashed Velázquez a smile that threatened for a moment to wrap him up in silk and race him through a *pasodoble* in a Ferrari.

Velázquez took out his ID and held it out to the girl, then saw her sexy manner wilt like a lily in a hurricane. 'I believe you had a call from a priest a little earlier?'

'That would be Father Pedro. He asked us to send a lad of ours over to keep him company–'

'The lad's name was Ramón, wasn't it?'

'That's right, but what's it to you?'

'I already showed you my ID.'

'That's right you did,' the girl said. 'But it doesn't explain why you want to know who our client asked for.'

'The badge means I get to ask the questions,' Velázquez said. 'All you have to do is answer them.'

'I prefer to go in for reciprocal relationships.'

'Seems to me you're working in the wrong place.'

'Is that supposed to be funny?'

'Give me this Ramón's full name and details.'

The girl shrugged and her chest shrugged along with her under her tight violet-coloured top. She looked at her computer screen, tapped a few keys, and scribbled on a pad. She tore the sheet off and handed it to Velázquez, then leaned her elbows on the wooden desk so that the Inspector Jefe got an eyeful. He looked at the address, then said, 'This chico Ramón offers sex in return for cash, I take it?'

The girl merely smiled at Velázquez. And kept smiling.

And her chest kept smiling along with her.

'What address was he asked to go to?'

The girl looked back at the screen, scribbled on the pad again and handed it to Velázquez. Father Pedro's address on Calle Viriato, as he had expected.

'Is Father Pedro a regular client?'

The girl shook her head. 'It was his first time with us.'

'Have you got a photo of Ramón?'

'I can print one off for you, if you like.'

'*Gracias.*'

The Inspector Jefe looked at the mug shot, then folded it and put the piece of paper in his pocket.

'Is there anything else I can do for you, Inspector Jefe?'

'I'll let you know if there is.'

He made for the door.

'Aren't you going to stick around?'

Velázquez said, 'Let's save it for a rainy day, shall we?' Then heard the girl say, 'Tomorrow's forecast is torrential rain, so don't leave the house without your mackintosh.'

Chapter 2

Inspector Jefe Velázquez tried the address the girl had given him for Ramón Ochoa, but nobody was home. He climbed back in his car and called Subinspector Gajardo. When Gajardo picked up, Velázquez said, 'Has our friend Ramón shown yet?'

''Fraid not, boss. What do you want me to do now?'

'Hook up with Serrano, Pérez and Merino, and see if they've turned up anything.'

'What've they been doing, boss?'

'Knocking on doors,' Velázquez said. 'You know the routine – make sure they've talked to all of the people who live in the building. If anyone was out when they called earlier, then they're to go back and try again. Once they've spoken to everyone in the block, get them to start calling on people in the neighbouring buildings. You can help them out. Try all the local shops, the butcher's and the green grocer's, any bars and cafes in the area. I want to know if anyone saw Father Pedro in the hours leading up to the time he was murdered. And try to find out what kind of man he was, what sort of company he kept, anything you can about his lifestyle…Oh, and give Javi the mug shot of Ramón Ochoa, and tell him to go round the gay bars. I want to know straightaway if anyone turns anything up.'

They hung up and, some forty minutes later, Velázquez hooked up with Gajardo and the rest of his team, in the building on Calle Viriato. It turned out that nobody the officers had spoken to heard or saw anything out of the ordinary.

Nobody recalled having seen any unfamiliar faces enter or leave the block in which Father Pedro lived, either.

Neither did anyone know whether or not Father Pedro had been gay. Some people had expressed a degree of surprise at the question, though. What did the man's sexuality have to do with anything? they wanted to know.

Besides, what did people see when they looked at a priest? What they wanted to, in most cases, Velázquez figured. Where

9

some people saw a servant of God, others saw a hated enemy. Even, in some cases, a servant of the Guy Downstairs.

Velázquez told his team to continue with what they had been doing, and began knocking on doors himself. He kept at it until well into the early hours of the morning, then figured he'd go and try Ramón's address once more. Again nobody came to the door when he rang the bell. Instead a little old lady in a dressing gown appeared in the doorway of the neighbouring flat. 'Pilar's not at home,' she said.

'Does she make a habit of staying out this late?'

The woman's head tilted to one side. 'You don't sound as though you know her all that well.'

Velázquez showed the woman his ID and introduced himself. The woman asked him if Ramon had got himself into trouble of some sort. The Inspector Jefe shook his head. 'Nothing like that,' he said. 'I just need to talk to him about an incident he may have been a witness to. It's just routine.'

'Pilar's a nurse over at the Macarena hospital, works nights some of the time.' The woman swept a hand blotched with liver spots over her gunmetal-grey hair. 'She won't be back until the morning, then she normally sleeps in until early in the afternoon.'

Velázquez glanced at his watch: it had just gone 2 a.m. Time to call it a night. He thanked the woman for her help, then left the building and walked through the narrow streets back to his car.

There were no parking spaces left when he got home, so he had to drive around searching for one. He ended up all the way down on Jesús del Gran Poder, by the colony of pimps, prostitutes and pushers.

He was feeling like shit as he entered the block on Calle Teodosio. He needed a fix. He ran up the stairs, let himself into the flat and shut the front door quietly, then padded along the hallway. Opening the door slowly, careful not to make a noise, he peered into the bedroom and saw that Ana was asleep. The light was still on and a book had fallen onto the floor by her side. Boy was she beautiful, with her long black hair all sprayed out on the pillow like that.

Returning to the living room, he took the baggie and syringe from their hiding place on the shelf, behind his selection of true-crime and history books. He went into the kitchen, put some of the heroin in a spoon and heated it up. Then he filled the syringe, rolled up his shirtsleeve and pumped his arm. He experienced a moment of intense pleasure when the needle went in.

Afterwards, he cleaned up then returned the baggie to its hiding place. He knew it was crazy, living like this. But it wasn't like he'd chosen to become an addict.

He had been abducted at gunpoint by an odd couple who called themselves Bill and the Black Lady. Quite who the pair were, Velázquez had yet to find out. But he was determined to do so, if it was the last thing he ever did. He suspected they had been working for someone that bore him a grudge.

They'd marked him, changed him in ways that he hadn't wanted to be changed. It would come back to him at night, and he'd wake up in a cold sweat, remembering. They had tied him to the chair, the Black Lady giving him all this spiel about coming over from New Orleans just for him. Bullshit, all of it. Velázquez doubted she was even 'black'. Not that he could see her, blindfolded as he was. The crazy pair had acted like it was all a big laugh for them, and he was the butt of the joke. Then the guy who called himself Bill would put the needle in, and everything started to be fun. For a while, anyway…

Velázquez told himself it might not be his fault he'd become an addict, but that didn't mean he couldn't do something about it.

He knew he couldn't carry on like this. He had to kick his habit. He'd go and see a doctor, and get some methadone. It was the only way.

He ran the cold-water tap and washed his face at the sink, then checked on Ana again, just to make sure she was still asleep.

What she didn't know couldn't hurt her.

He found the bottle of single malt in the drinks cabinet and poured himself a large one. He kicked his loafers off, threw his jacket over the back of a chair and sat on the leather sofa with his feet up on the glass coffee table. He sipped his single malt

11

and ran through the details of the case in his mind, trying to work out what might have happened. He kept wondering if there were some line of inquiry he'd overlooked.

It was coming up to 3:30 a.m. when Velázquez finally turned in, and he slept fitfully. The crime scene featured in his dreams, only somehow everything was transformed.

The alarm went off at 7:30 a.m. Velázquez got up, washed and dressed, then drank a strong coffee before he left the flat. He found the Seat Ibiza parked where he'd left it, started her up and set off.

Seville is always beautiful, but at this hour, before the traffic of the day had begun to clog the streets, the city seemed to be full of subtle and ancient mysteries. He drove past the Maestranza bullring and the Torre de Oro, before he crossed the bridge and then headed up Blas Infante to the Jefatura. He slotted his car into the bay allocated to him in the underground car park, then took the lift up.

Serrano, Pérez and Merino were working at their desks when Velázquez entered the office. He said '*Buenos días*' and sat at his desk, then booted up his computer. Minutes later, Gajardo came in. 'Okay,' Velázquez said, 'now everyone's here you'd all better drop everything and get out and pick up where you left off last night.'

Jorge Serrano blew out his freckled cheeks, then ran a chubby hand through his receding ginger hair.

'Don't look so excited, Jorge.'

'Sorry, boss, it's just that –'

'You don't like going out knocking on doors, prefer to be doing something else, I know. So would everyone else. Knocking on doors isn't exciting. You don't see Mel Gibson do a whole lot of it in Lethal Weapon. But just because Hollywood can't find any space for it doesn't mean to say it hasn't got to be done. Do I make myself clear?'

'*Sí*, boss.' Serrano got up from his chair and stretched his arms.

Noticing the dark patches of sweat under the arms in Jorge's blue guayabera, Velázquez wondered when the air con in the officer was going to be fixed. Then he said, 'Come on, the four of you. Let's show Clint Eastwood and Mel Gibson how to do it.' He paused for a moment, and grinned at his team. 'Get out there and make my day.'

The Inspector Jefe drove at a slow crawl through heavy traffic over to Forensics, which was situated in a large building on Avenida Doctor Fedriani. Once inside the building, he tracked down Raúl Almonte, head of the Científico team. Almonte was a short skinny guy with a big ego, and he was dressed in what Velázquez thought of as a 'space suit', the usual getup the officers in the Policía Científico team wore when they were going about their work, only he had taken his headgear off in order to talk.

To Velázquez's way of thinking, Raúl Almonte acted like it was all down to him and his team whether any murder cases got solved, and this rubbed the Inspector Jefe up the wrong way even though he did his best to hide the fact.

He asked Almonte if he and his team had managed to turn anything up yet, and the man shook his head. 'As I'm sure you already know, Inspector Jefe, there was no sign of the gun, or of whatever it was the killer hit the victim on the back of the head with.' He shrugged. 'Which gives us a whole lot of nothing to work with.'

Velázquez held the knife up in its plastic wrapping, and took a good look at it. 'It's a standard bread knife,' he said. He wondered if the killer had brought it to the crime scene or found it in the kitchen. 'Is it okay if I take it with me?'

'Sure.' Almonte shrugged. 'I've finished with it here.'

Velázquez went down to the dissecting lab, where he found Gómez stooped over the body of the murder victim.

'*Buenos días*, Juan. It looks like you're busy.'

'You know what they say, Luis,' Gómez said. 'No rest for the wicked and all that.'

'Starting to sound like a priest.'

Gómez looked up at Velázquez over the steel frame of his glasses, perched on his rather sizeable nose. 'God forbid.'

Velázquez glanced at the body of the victim on the dissecting table, already cut open from throat to pelvis. 'Don't be shy,' Gómez said. 'Take a good look. That's what we're all made of. Any one of these vital organs packs up and we pack up with it.'

'That's a happy thought.'

Gómez went back to digging around inside the body. 'The bullet's been sent down to Ballistics, in case you're wondering, Luis,' he said without looking up.

'Is there any evidence of intercourse having taken place?'

Gómez shook his head. 'There's an indentation on the back of the skull, consistent with a hard blow from a solid blunt instrument. But you already know that.'

'I've got to go.'

'We must have a drink sometime.'

'I'll call you.'

Velázquez drove back to the crime scene. He parked with two wheels up on the narrow pavement on Calle Viriato, which was already packed with parked cars and pedestrians. The sun was shining out of a clear blue sky. It wasn't really hot yet, but it soon would be.

He let himself into the building with the spare key he'd had made, and slipped on a pair of nitrile gloves as he went up the stairs. Once he had entered the flat, he made straight for the kitchen. He opened the cutlery drawer and emptied its contents out onto the Formica worktop.

He took all the knives he could find and put them into a carrier bag, then left. He headed off on foot down to the end of Viriato, then turned up Amor de Dios and traversed the Plaza del Duque, where tourists were sitting on the benches feeding the pigeons. He entered the Corte Ingles, which was the best place to buy just about anything as long as you didn't mind paying full whack for it.

He made straight for the cutlery department, and explained to the manager what he needed to find out. The man made a brief examination, then said that the knife in the plastic bag was part of a set along with several of the other knives the Inspector Jefe had brought with him.

'Do you sell a set like this here?'

'Yes we do, as a matter of fact.' The man came out from behind the counter and led Velázquez along one of the aisles. He stopped and pointed to a set that was on display. 'Here.'

'You mean to say this is the very same set?'

'It is indeed.' The man reached out and took a long bread knife from the box. 'And this is the same model of knife as the one you showed me.'

Velázquez drove over to Ramón Ochoa's address once again. A woman in her fifties, dressed in jeans and a pink T-shirt, came to the door. She said, '*Hola*,' and looked at Velázquez out of tired brown eyes underscored by dark bags.

'Are you Señora Pilar Ochoa, Ramón's mother?'

'That's right...but why are you asking?'

Velázquez took out his ID and held it up. Señora Ochoa squinted at it. 'What d'you want with my Ramón?'

'Just to talk to him, that's all.'

'Well, he's not here.'

'Any idea when he'll be back?'

Pilar Ochoa shrugged. 'I haven't seen him for a few days.'

'Where's he gone?'

'No idea.'

'Is that usual for him – to disappear for a few days at a time?'

'He's a grown man of twenty-five, comes and goes as he pleases.'

'Has he got a partner, or anyone he hangs out with?'

'Nobody he's told me about.'

Velázquez figured a little improvisation was needed. 'Look, Señora Ochoa, I have reason to believe your son's life may be in danger.'

The woman's brown eyes flashed like she'd just woken up. 'What makes you say that?'

'A friend of his has been murdered.'

Her mouth opened, and her hand moved to cover it in an automatic gesture. 'What's the name of this friend?'

'He's a priest by the name of Father Pedro Mora, and whoever it was that killed him may well come after Ramón, too.'

'Why'd they be after Ramón?'

'We have reason to believe the priest was gay,' Velázquez lied. 'And, as I say, that he was friendly with your son.'

Pilar Ochoa frowned, chewing on her lower lip. 'So you think the killer might've been someone who hates gays, is that it?'

'That's one line of inquiry we're considering.'

The woman looked into Velázquez's eyes, as if she were trying to decide whether or not to trust him. Then she said, 'There's a bar that Ramón goes to a lot, over on Calle Betis…Jorge's, I think it's called.'

Velázquez thanked the woman for her help. 'And if he comes back then please ask him to give me a call on this number,' he said, and handed her his card.

Velázquez called his number two, but Gajardo wasn't answering for some reason. The Inspector Jefe hung up then called Jorge Serrano. When Jorge answered, Velàzquez asked him if he had turned up anything of interest yet.

'The victim played golf during the morning, boss, at a club near Jerez,' Serrano said in his clear-cut Madrid accent.

'Who did he play with?'

'A German guy by the name of Moeller.'

'Spoken to him yet?'

'I'm on my way to the man's flat now.'

'Find out everything you can about the man.'

'Will do, boss.'

'Is Subinspector Gajardo with you?'

'He's gone to the golf club, to see if he can turn up anything of interest down there.'

'What about Pérez and Merino?'

'They're still knocking on doors.'

'Okay, Jorge, I'll catch you later. And let me know straightaway if you turn anything up.'

'Sure.'

'And be at the Jefatura by three this afternoon. Tell the others, too. I need you all there for a briefing.'

Chapter 3

Velázquez climbed into the Seat Ibiza and set off through the heavy traffic for the Jefatura on Blas Infante. Normally he didn't mind driving around Seville, but lately it had become something of a pain. He was missing his old car, the one that had been stolen, the Alfa Romeo. His Alfa Romeo. Somehow he was nostalgic for it today, and the fact that he knew his feelings were ridiculous and pointless did nothing to diminish them.

Gajardo, Serrano and Merino were in the office, working at their desks, when Velázquez arrived. He said hello to everyone and shrugged his black linen jacket off, then draped it over the back of his chair, before he booted up his computer. He had just started writing his report when he heard Pérez's familiar voice say '*Buenos días.*' Like Jorge, Sara spoke with a Madrid accent, the pair of them having moved down here to enter the Department after passing the state exams or oposiciones. At first Velázquez had wondered whether they would find it difficult to settle, coming from the capital as they did; but here they both were, still working in his team, over twenty years later.

Pérez was a tall brunette and, at forty-six, still attractive enough to turn heads when she walked down the street or entered a restaurant. Today she was wearing a grey trouser suit done in cotton, and she now took the jacket off and hung it on the peg over on the wall.

'Okay, everyone,' Velázquez said, 'now you're all here, let me have your attention.' He got up from his chair and went over to the whiteboard. 'You don't need me to tell you that we're up against a real sicko on this one. And there's nothing to say he won't strike again soon, so we'll be working long hours until we catch him. I'm afraid our loved ones are just going to have to show a little patience.' He picked up the black marker pen and took off the cap. 'Now let's stick to the facts and look at what we know.'

He turned to face the whiteboard. At the side of the mug shot of the victim that had been pinned there, he drew a line at ten o'clock. 'Our victim goes down to El Soleo Golf Club outside Jerez and is seen playing golf.' He looked at Gajardo. 'Correct, Subinspector?'

'That's right, boss.'

'Would you care to fill us in on anything else you learned while you were down there?'

'The victim played a round with a German by the name of Gerhardt Moeller. Both men are well into their seventies, which may explain why they chose to play against each other.'

'Is there anything else you can tell us?'

'They started playing around ten in the morning and finished their round shortly before noon.'

'Okay.' Velázquez drew another line at twelve o'clock. He added a vertical line to connect the two lines he had previously drawn. Then he wrote PLAYED GOLF WITH GERHARDT MOELLER along it. 'Were they joined by a third party?'

'There was no third party, boss.'

Velázquez turned back to Serrano. 'You spoke to Moeller, Jorge. What sort of impression did he make on you?'

'Seemed like a pretty normal kind of old guy.'

'Normal, huh?'

'*Si*.' Serrano shrugged his heavy shoulders.

'That doesn't tell us a lot, Agente. I think we can do better than that.'

Serrano frowned. 'The guy's German but speaks good Spanish, only with an accent.'

'Do we know where he lives yet?'

'He's got a small flat off Calle Feria.'

'What job did the man do before he retired?'

'He said he used to work in a bank and that he got to know Father Pedro through the church.'

'What time did he last see Father Pedro?'

'He says he parted company with him shortly after two p.m. They had lunch together at the Sardinero, a bar on the *plaza* outside the Iglesia del Gran Poder. Moeller claims they said goodbye there. Moeller picked up the tab and Father Pedro disappeared into the church.'

'Have you managed to get anyone to corroborate that?'

'A waiter that works at the Sardinero remembered serving them.'

'What time would this have been?'

'The waiter couldn't be totally exact about the time, but said he knew it was before quarter past two because that was when he left work. He said he had an appointment at the dentist's, which is a short walk from the Sardinero, at two-thirty. He remembered seeing the two men go their separate ways. And he confirmed it was like Moeller said – that Father Pedro went into the church and Moeller went off in the other direction, across the square.'

'And where did Moeller go then?'

'He claims he walked back to his flat and stayed there until late in the evening.'

'How late?'

'Just gone ten.'

'By which time the victim was long dead,' Javier Merino said.

Velázquez looked at Merino, a skinny man of twenty-five with short black hair, and nodded. 'Have you managed to corroborate any of this, Jorge?'

'Only his movements up until he left the Sardinero, boss.'

'Which could make Moeller a suspect, are we thinking, or what?' Sara Pérez wanted to know.

'Sure he's a suspect,' Velázquez said. 'So is just about everyone else in this damn city.' He looked at Serrano. 'What about Father Pedro? Can we account for his movements after that?'

'He talked to a Father Antonio for a while in the church. Father Antonio says Father Pedro left the church around four p.m., after telling him he was going home.'

'Then what?'

Serrano shrugged, and his freckled brow creased in a frown. 'Then nothing, boss...until he was murdered.'

'That's the gap we need to fill.' Velázquez wrote more timelines with events on the whiteboard. Then he pointed at what he'd just written. 'The gap in time between Father Pedro's leaving the Iglesia de Jesús del Gran Poder and the time he was killed.'

'Which was when exactly did we say again, boss?' Javi Merino asked.

'We didn't…but the body was still warm, suggesting that the murder had taken place no more than an hour before we arrived on the scene.'

'And you arrived at the flat shortly before eight,' Sara Pérez said. 'So we need to account for Father Pedro's movements between around four in the afternoon and sometime before eight p.m.'

'Exactly…those four hours.' Velázquez cleared his throat, then he looked at Subinspector Gajardo. 'How did the two men get on playing golf together, José?'

'Father Pedro won, boss…finished with a birdie by all accounts. It sounds like he's a pretty useful player – bloody amazing when you consider the man's age.'

'That might've been a motive for revenge,' Agent Serrano said.

Velázquez permitted himself a restrained grin. 'With sports psychology like that, Jorge, I can see I'd better not play you at pool.'

Chapter 4

Velázquez climbed into the Seat Ibiza and called his wife Ana on his mobile, to tell her he would be home later than expected. But they had the de la Spadas coming over for dinner, Ana protested. Had he forgotten?

Velázquez hadn't forgotten. Juan de la Spada was one of the most successful bull-breeders in the business, while his wife was an up and coming actress. Which explained why the couple's comings and goings had recently become material for the gossip columns. But the Inspector Jefe found the prospect of having dinner with them no less boring for all that. Ana would be all right, because Laura de la Spada was cultured and capable of making conversation. Velázquez could picture the two women getting along like a house on fire. But as for himself, he would be forced to listen to yet another lecture from Juan de la Spada on how he bred his bulls.

'It's just that there's been a murder, Ana–a particularly nasty and brutal one.'

'I said I'd be serving dinner at ten, so they should come over at nine-thirty,' she said. 'You'd better not let me down, Luis.'

'Okay, I'll be there. *Te quiero.*'

'I love you, too.'

Velázquez started up the engine and drove over to Jorge's, the bar that Pilar Ochoa had told him about. The place was full when he got there, and he had to squeeze between huddles of drinkers to get to the counter.

He asked the barman, a muscled guy in a black T-shirt, if he knew a Ramón Ochoa. The man shrugged. Loads of people came in this place, he said. And some of them were called Ramón. It was a fairly common name, after all, and customers didn't necessarily make a habit of telling everyone their surnames. 'People come here to relax,' he said. 'It's an informal kind of place, y'know?'

Velázquez showed the man the photograph the girl at the agency had given him.

The barman looked at the photo and frowned. 'Can I ask why you're looking for him?'

'I think his life may well be in serious danger.'

'Are you a cop?'

Velázquez nodded and flashed his ID.

'What kind of danger?'

'A friend of his has been murdered.'

The man's bushy eyebrows rose. 'What friend would this be?'

'Look, I haven't got time to waste.'

'He was in here last night, as it happens.'

'Did he leave with anyone?'

The man leaned over the counter and pointed across the crowded bar. 'See the tall blond guy over by the wall,' he said. 'The one that's wearing far too much makeup, and an excuse for a dress?'

Velázquez nodded.

'His name's Clara. You might try askin' him.'

Velázquez crossed the bar, squeezing through the huddles of drinkers. The clientele was made up of a medley of leathers and shaved heads sporting peaked policeman's caps, Freddy Mercury moustaches, and drag. Velázquez made eye contact with the man the barman had pointed out. '*Hola*, you're Clara, I believe?'

'That's right. Don't tell me you've heard of me? All good, I hope?' The man was wearing a skimpy red number, fishnet stockings, killer heels, a blond wig and scarlet lipstick. But despite all of the trouble he'd taken, he still looked like a guy in a dress.

Velázquez flashed his ID. The man, Clara, looked at it then shrugged. 'I haven't done anything. Although I might be up for a little undercover work later, honey, if you're in the mood to tango.'

'I've always been more of a foxtrot man, I'm afraid.' Velázquez held up the photograph. 'I'm looking for this man. His name's Ramón Ochoa. Somebody told me you know him.'

'I know all sorts of people, honey,'

'He was in this place last night.'

'What if he was?'

'I've reason to believe he could be in serious danger,' Velázquez said. 'Now did you see him here last night?'

Clara nodded.

'Was he with anybody?'

'He left with an English chico by the name of Eric Waters. Eric's a skinny guy with short blond hair and far too many spots for my liking.'

'Do you know where this Eric Waters lives?'

'No, but he teaches at the Escuela de Idiomas.'

'How do you know where he works?'

'It was me that introduced him to Ramón. I used to be one of his students.'

'Is that the school over on Avenida Doctor Fedriani?'

'That's right. It doesn't shut 'til around nine, so if you go there now you might just catch him.

'*Gracias.*'

'And don't forget to go prepared, Inspector,' Clara said. 'Because there's a nasty serial killer out there on the loose, in case you hadn't heard.'

'Are you trying to tell me something?'

'AIDS, honey.' Clara smiled. 'Be sure to take a condom with you, wherever it is you're headed.'

Velázquez showed the young receptionist at the Escuela de Idiomas his ID, and told her he needed to speak to an Eric Waters that taught there. The girl glanced at her watch. 'As it happens, he should just be finishing his class,' she said. 'Come with me.'

The students were packing their things away as they entered the classroom. The receptionist told Waters he had a visitor, and Velázquez quickly introduced himself, holding up his ID as he did so.

Waters looked like a student himself, from the skinny frame and clothes – grey Levi's, blue Vans, plain white T-shirt – down to the fresh acne scars on his jaw and neck. 'It's about your

24

friend Ramon Ochoa,' Velázquez said. 'I think he may be in some kind of trouble and I want to help him.'

'Why? What's happened?'

'There's no time to explain. I need to find Ramón. Have you any idea where he is?'

'I left him at my place before I came over here.' Eric spoke with an accent that was about as Spanish as egg, bacon and beans for breakfast.

'What time was that?'

'I must've left home about twenty to six.'

'We're talking p.m., are we?'

'That's right.'

'When did Ramón show at your place?'

'Not very long before I left.'

'Can you be more precise?'

'He must've shown at around twenty-past five, give or take a few minutes.'

'So why'd he stay there if you were leaving?'

'He'd spent the night at mine, then left in the morning and couldn't find his mobile. He reckoned he probably left it behind.'

'Did he find it?'

Eric shrugged his narrow shoulders. 'He was still looking for it when I left.'

'Do you think there's any chance he's still there?'

'I guess that depends on whether or not he's found it.'

'Are you going there now?'

'No, I've got to teach a couple of private lessons after I leave this place, and then I'm going to meet some friends.'

'What's your address?'

'Why do you ask?'

'In case I need to speak to you again,' Velázquez said. 'Just routine.'

'Number twenty Calle Correduría, flat 3B.'

Velázquez made a note of it before he said, 'What sort of mood was Ramón in when you left him?'

'He seemed pretty agitated.'

'Any idea why that might've been?'

'How would you feel in his shoes?'

'Huh?'

'It was an Apple,' Eric Waters said. 'Those things don't come cheap.'

Velázquez parked in one of the side streets off the Alameda de Hercules, then went in search of Calle Correduría. But he couldn't find the street, so he asked an old man for directions. The man pointed with his walking stick: it was just the other side of the Alameda. Velázquez thanked the man, and set off across the muddy stretch of rubble-strewn expanse.

A girl wearing a tatty handkerchief for a skirt came over and asked him if he'd like to have some fun. He glanced at her without slackening his pace, and the girl did her best to crack an appealing smile. Velázquez caught sight of the orthodontic nightmare she had for teeth. He told her he was a 'poli' and the girl said in that case he could have it for half price. 'I'm sure you can charge it to your expense account, darlin'.'

He pressed on and soon found himself on Correduria, one of the side streets that run from the Alameda up to Calle Feria. The building Eric Waters lived in was up near the next corner, a tall, nondescript affair from the outside. Velázquez pushed a random button on the console, and somebody buzzed him in without bothering to ask who was calling.

There was no lift, so he ran up the stairs and found the door to the flat. It had been left ajar. He knocked on the panelled wood, but nobody came. He tried the buzzer. There was still no sign of anybody, so he went in through the door.

He found himself in a dark hallway, and there was some kind of crazy music playing. Flamenco meets Sid Vicious. '*Hola*?' Velázquez called out. 'Is anybody home?'

Nobody answered.

He pressed the light switch. Nothing happened.

Then something, or somebody, hit him on the back of the head…

When Velázquez came round, minutes later, the back of his head hurt like a bastard. He shat in the milk as he rubbed the place where he'd been hit. Quite a lump had formed there. But where was he? And who had hit him?

It took Velázquez a moment to remember that he was in Eric Waters' place. Having established that much, he remembered that he'd come here in the hope of finding Ramón Ochoa.

He figured it must have been Ochoa that took him by surprise with a blow from behind, in which case the man would be long gone.

Velázquez searched the flat anyway, as a matter of course, but he didn't find anyone home.

He wondered whether Ochoa was the killer.

He figured that was a possibility.

But it was just as possible that Ochoa might have taken fright at the idea of being charged with murder, and had decided to do whatever he could to avoid being arrested.

Velázquez left the building and walked the short distance back to his flat on Calle Teodosio.

Ana was in the kitchen, doing the dishes, when Velázquez finally got home at just after 2 a.m., and she gave him a look that would have stopped a bull in its tracks. 'It's nice of you to show at last,' she said. 'I appreciate the courtesy, even though you're a few hours late for dinner.'

'I can explain, Ana.'

'You always can…that's half the problem.'

'You don't know what happened.'

'No.' She sighed and her beautiful black eyes flashed. 'But I'm sure it'll make a good story.' She looked at him, hands on hips, every molecule in her body somehow working to show just how pissed off she was. 'Come on,' she said. 'Shock me…tell me how you threw the house through the window to make sure you'd get here on time, even though you still didn't make it. What was it this time? Don't tell me. Some psycho of a gangster turned his pet Komodo dragon loose on you. One lash of its tongue'd be enough to kill a man forty times over. So you jumped on its back and wrestled with it, until you finally killed it, and then came rushing home to your blushing damsel of a bullfighter wife, to boast. Am I right?'

27

'Not quite.'

'Maybe it was a pet crocodile, then. Or better still, a pool full of piranha fish? Four seconds in the water and there'd've been nothing left of you but your shoe laces.'

'You're forgetting something, Ana.'

'What?'

'I'm wearing slip-ons.'

The following morning, Velázquez dialled the number for the Escuela de Idiomas. A pleasant female voice answered. Velázquez explained who he was and asked to speak to Eric Waters. 'It's urgent,' he said.

'I'm sorry, but Eric phoned in sick today.'

'*Gracias.*' Velázquez hung up and headed out of the office, stopping at the door only to tell the members of his team he needed them out knocking on doors again.

The Inspector Jefe took the lift down to the basement car park, found his car and set off for Eric Waters' place. He pulled up minutes later on Calle Correduría, and stepped out onto the cobbled street.

He hadn't gone far before a man approached him. In his faded jeans, white string vest and shades, the character had dealer written all over him. 'Need a wrap?' Velázquez was about to tell the man he was a 'poli', but then he had another idea. 'I'll take a couple.' The coast was clear–he'd checked. 'Ten thousand *pesetas.*' Velázquez tried to knock him down, but the bastard laughed in his face.

Just then, a squad car turned the corner, and Velázquez felt his heart thumping in his chest. 'Okay,' he said. 'But quick about it – here come the polis.'

The exchange was made just before the squad car drew up. The uniform sitting in the passenger seat looked out at Velázquez, and the Inspector Jefe told the man who he was and flashed his ID. 'I was just talking to an informant of mine,' he said. The uniform nodded, then said, 'Have a good day,' and the car went on its way.

Velázquez breathed a sigh of relief. He was an idiot to go buying heroin in the street like that. Especially round here. The

Alameda de Hercules was a magnet for cops, after all. It would be safer to go out to the Tres Mil Viviendas to buy the stuff. Police rarely went there, unless they were on a raid.

Velázquez found the door to the building where Eric Waters lived and pushed a button on the console at random. A woman's voice asked him who he was. Velázquez told her he'd come to fix the plumbing.

'There's nothing wrong with my plumbing,' the woman said.

'No, it's on the floor below. Sorry, I pushed the wrong button.'

The woman buzzed him in. Not wanting to go through a repeat of his last visit, Velázquez took his gun out as he ran up the stairs. He slowed down as he reached the third floor.

This time the door was locked. He pushed the buzzer. Nothing doing. He pushed it again.

Nobody was in.

Or if they were, then they weren't in a very sociable mood. Velázquez took out his lock picks and got the door open, then entered the flat, holding his gun out in front of him. He found the light switch and pressed it. Nothing happened. Then he noticed the television was on over in the corner of the room. On the screen, a blond guy was fellating another man. The sound was turned off.

Glancing up at the ceiling, Velázquez noticed there was no bulb. Perhaps Ramón took it out, to give himself the advantage in the event of a surprise visit. The shutters were partially drawn and the light that filtered in, combined with that from the television, was just enough for Velázquez to be able to see by.

He moved forward into the room, holding his gun up and crouching like a hunter stalking his prey. A short hallway led off the living room, and there were three doors in it. He kicked the first one open, and found himself looking at a toilet and a sink.

Nobody was in there.

He kicked the door to his right, then took a quick look in. There was a double bed, unmade, with nobody in it. That just left the second door on the left.

Velázquez kicked that open too, and found himself looking at a bathtub that doubled up as a shower. He tore the screen back.

Nobody.

Chapter 5

Velázquez called in to Jorge's early in the afternoon. To his surprise, the place seemed to be doing a fairly good trade, despite the hour. No sooner had he got to the counter than Clara came over to him: 'Hello, sailor.'

'I'm not a sailor. I'm a poli.'

'Every guy in this place is a sailor, far as I'm concerned, hon.'

Velázquez smiled and said, 'Whatever floats your boat.' He turned to the barman. 'I'll have a beer. And whatever Clara wants.'

'I'd better not say what I really really want, hon, because it's dirty. But I'll settle for a large glass of Chablis.' Clara dug into his gold-coloured handbag and brought out a packet of Camels. He took a cigarette from the pack and lit up, then had himself a long drag that looked like it hurt. He exhaled twin columns of smoke through his large nostrils, before offering Velázquez the pack.

Velazquez declined with a shake of the head. 'I gave up.'

'I like a man with will power.'

'I'm still looking for Ramón Ochoa.'

Clara sipped his Chablis. 'Sound like you got it bad, hon. And that ain't good.' He took another agonized drag on his Camel. 'What's this Ramón got that I haven't?'

'Information.'

'You should check out the mine of info I got down my knickers, hon.'

The door opened, and Eric Waters came in with another man. Clara said, 'Talk of the devil – there there he is. Seems like it could be your lucky day.'

Velázquez hadn't recognized Ochoa. His face seemed longer than it was in his mug shot, and it looked like someone had left the man's nose wondering which way was north. He had his hair tied back in a ponytail –another new touch – and could have done with a shave.

The man made his way over to the counter, and Velázquez approached him. 'I've been looking for you, Ramon.' The Inspector Jefe took out his ID and flashed it.

Ochoa's brown eyes were full of bitter derision. 'Well I sure ain't been looking for you.'

'We need to talk.'

'You might, but I'm here to have a drink.'

'I'm not sure I like your manners.'

'Who said you were meant to?'

The barman placed Ramón's beer down on the counter. He picked it up and took a sip, then leered at Velázquez and belched in his face.

'You can either come down to the Jefatura with me now, of your own accord, Ramón,' Velázquez said, 'or I can arrest you.'

'I ain't done nothing.'

'Why did you hit me on the head last night?'

'*Que*?'

'Come on,' Velázquez said, 'stop bullshitting me. I know it was you.'

'I've never seen you before.'

'At Eric Waters' place…you came at me from behind and took me by surprise.'

'You're crazy.'

'Now as I just said, you can either come down to the Jefatura of your own accord or I can arrest you. Which is it to be?'

'Arrest me? You must have the wrong man. I already told you I ain't done nothing.'

'Not unless you count a little matter like committing a murder.'

'What? Are you kidding me? Who the fuck'm I suppose to've killed?'

'Father Pedro Mora.'

Ramón threw his drink in Velázquez's face, then turned and made a dash for it. Velázquez gave chase, but tripped over an outstretched foot. By the time he got outside there was no sign of Ramón Ochoa.

Velázquez called Agente Serrano and explained what had just happened. 'I need you to go over to Ramón Ochoa's mother's place and see if he's there.'

'Sure. You got an address, boss?'

Velázquez read it out to him from his notebook.

'And what if he's not there?'

'Scour every gay bar in the city,' Velázquez said. 'Talk to people and see if you can find anyone who knows him or might've seen him. Take Merino and Pérez with you.'

'I could do with a copy of the mug shot, boss.'

'Ask Subinspector Gajardo to get you a copy. And contact me straightaway if you find him.'

They hung up and Velázque made a tour of the gay bars without catching sight of Ramón Ochoa. Then he drove over to the Escuela de Idiomas, where he told the receptionist he needed to speak to Eric Waters. The woman said Eric was teaching a class. 'This is a matter of some importance,' Velázquez said, and showed her his ID. 'Perhaps you'd like to go and get him for me.' He smiled. 'Unless you'd prefer me to go in and get him myself?

'If you'd just like to wait here a moment.' The girl went off and returned moments later with Eric Waters.

'Oh, it's you again.' Waters said.

'Don't sound so pleased to see me, Eric.'

'This is getting to be a bad habit.'

'I won't take up much of your time,' Velázquez said. 'I'm sure it won't come as any great surprise if I tell you I'm looking for your friend Ramón Ochoa.'

'I haven't seen him since I was in Jorge's with him, earlier, and you were there.'

'Any idea where he might have gone?

Eric Waters shrugged. 'How should I know? I mean, it's not like we're not married – '

'If you see him, can I trust you to call me?'

'Yes, of course,' Waters said. 'Now if that's all, I hope you won't mind if I go back to my class. They've got an exam next Wednesday and half of them still know as much about the Perfect tenses as I do about a nun's – '

'Please pass on my apologies to your students, will you,' Velázquez said, turning to leave. 'You might also tell them that I managed to pass my exams in English, and I don't know the first thing about nuns, either.'

As he drove through the streets, Velázquez took out his mobile and called Serrano. 'What's new, Jorge?'

'I'm talking to Ochoa's mother at her flat right now.'

'And?'

'She says she hasn't seen or heard from him in days.'

'Tell Merino to stay on watch outside the front door to the block in his car,' the Inspector Jefe said. 'And you and Pérez can carry on looking for him.'

'Right you are, boss.'

Velázquez was feeling awful again by now. He needed a fix, so he headed back to his flat. And when he got in, he was surprised to find that Ana wasn't at home. Then he remembered she'd told him she had arranged to meet one of her old friends, Carmen López, for a drink.

After he'd shot up, he took a minute or two to relish the experience, before he hid the baggie in its usual hiding place. Then he went back out in search of Ramón Ochoa.

And failed to catch a whiff of the man.

He called Gajardo and learned from him that none of the other officers in the team had managed to turn up anything useful, either.

He decided to call it a day and returned home. Ana was sitting on the sofa reading a novel when he got in, having returned from wherever she'd gone to meet her old friend. She looked at him and asked how his day had been.

Instead of answering her question, Velázquez made straight for the drinks cabinet. 'Fancy joining me in one?'

'Was your day that bad?' Ana asked him. When she didn't get an answer, she shrugged and said, 'Go on, then. Put a dash of water in mine.'

He came over with the drinks and sat next to her on the leather sofa. Ana took hers and they clinked glasses. 'Your health,' Velázquez said and took a sip of his Scotch.

'Salud!' Ana set her book down on the coffee table.

Velázquez glanced at the cover: Libra by Don DeLillo. 'Any good?' he asked.

She nodded. 'It's about Lee Harvey Oswald and the assassination of JFK.'

Trust Ana to read about something like that, Velázquez thought. The police balls-up to end all police balls-ups. He picked the book up and read the blurb on the back cover. 'Sounds interesting,' he said, and put it back down. He kicked off his loafers. 'What sort of a day have you had, Ana?'

'I went out to the ranch and practised.'

'And how did it go?'

'Pretty well,' she said. 'You won't have forgotten that I'm on the bill up at Antequera tomorrow evening, I hope?'

'Of course not.' Velázquez smiled. 'I'm looking forward to it.' In truth, he was dreading it, as he dreaded all of Ana's bullfights.

'I just hope they give me some decent bulls to work with.'

Velázquez tapped twice on the pinewood coffee table. Ana laughed. 'For a cop you're not half superstitious.'

'What's being a cop got to do with it?'

'Cops are supposed to be methodical and rational, aren't they?'

Velázquez shrugged. 'All I know is we're supposed to catch the bad guys.' He watched Ana run a hand through her long mane of wavy black hair and marvelled again that a woman as beautiful as she was should have chosen to carve out a career for herself fighting bulls. He knew better than to tell her this, though. Instead, he told her how lovely she looked.

She smiled and asked him if he'd made any progress on the investigation.

'I finally caught up with the murder suspect.'

'Oh, that's good.'

'Then I let him get away.'

'Not so good after all, then,' she said. 'But are you sure he's the killer?'

'Right now, I'm not sure about anything.'

'Perhaps it's not such a bad thing that he got away, then.'

'That's what I love about you, Ana.'

'*Que*?'

'The way you can take a twenty-four-carat cock-up I've made and put a positive spin on it.' He shrugged. 'Anyway, I'll catch up with him before too long. Seville might be a fairly big city, but its criminal underworld is a village. And it's one in which everyone knows everyone else.'

'Do you mind if we leave that particular village behind for a while?'

They fell silent and sat gazing into each other's eyes. Then Ana said, 'Is that the only thing?'

'Huh?'

'That you love about me?' She ran her finger over his lips. 'You said you love the way I have of putting a positive spin on your cock-ups.'

'No, that's not the only thing I love about you.'

'So what are the other things?'

'Do you want a list, Ana?'

'I was kinda hoping you might be able to think of a more exciting way of communicating it than that, Luis.'

Afterwards, they sat sipping their drinks as they watched the news. They were both feeling pacified by the release of the storm cloud of hot febrile passion that had built up between them.

There was a report on the rising unemployment figures. Then they listened to a report on the murder of Father Pedro Mora. 'So far the police have made no arrests,' the newscaster said.

Velázquez picked up the control unit and posted the newscaster into orbit. 'Let's go to bed,' he said.

He fell asleep as soon as his head hit the pillow, and slipped straight into an old recurring nightmare. He was in a dark underground car park, and there was nobody else about. Or at least, so he'd thought, until he climbed into his beloved old Alfa

Romeo – and somebody hit him from behind. When he came round, he found that his knees were pushing up in his chest and his hands were tied. He tried to shout but there was a gag in his mouth.

His heart was hammering in his ears. He was terrified.

I'm in the boot of a car, he thought.

He heard sirens and figured his luck was in, then the sirens developed an odd tendency to ring. What the…He opened his eyes. His bedside telephone was ringing.

He reached out with a fumbling hand, and picked it up. '*Hola*?'

'Velázquez? Comisario Alonso here.' And Velázquez could tell from the man's tone that he had the bad milk.

'Another body's turned up. This fucking city's turning into an abattoir.'

'Where did it happen, Comisario?' Velázquez asked, reaching for the notepad and pen he always kept handy by the phone.

Comisario Alonso told him the address and he wrote it down.

'I've just had the mayor on the phone,' the Comisario said. 'He chewed my ear off about the damage to the tourist trade. Have you got any idea how much money these murders could cost this city, if we can't catch the killer quickly, Velázquez?'

'Do you want me to investigate this case, Comisario? Or d'you want me to do the PR for the Tourist Board?' Velázquez felt like saying.

But somehow he managed to bite his tongue.

Chapter 6

The frogmen had already got the body out of the river by the time Velázquez arrived on the scene, and somebody had checked through the victim's pockets. A wallet had been found. Velázquez looked through it and found various cards, including the victim's *carné* or ID card.

He halted the progress of two ambulance men carrying the body on a stretcher, and pulled back the sheet. Another dog collar. The body was lying on its side, so that Velázquez could see the face in profile. It was familiar to him. A kitchen knife of the kind that had been used on Father Pedro Mora was sticking out of the victim's backside.

The Inspector Jefe dropped the sheet, and allowed the ambulance men to go on their way. He asked the uniform that had given him the wallet if he knew who discovered the body. 'A night shift worker on his way home,' the officer said. 'He saw it floating on the water as he was crossing the bridge.'

At that moment Gajardo came hurrying over. 'Another priest, is it, boss?'

Velázquez nodded. 'A Father Aloysius,' he said. 'I talked to him when I went to the Iglesia de Jesús del Gran Poder about Father Mora. The two men were friends.'

'Looks like we're dealing with someone who's got a serious grudge against priests, boss,' the Subinspector said. 'What about the modus operandi?'

'It appears to've been the same as the one used on Father Pedro.'

'The bullet and the kitchen knife?'

'I don't know yet whether he was shot, but a kitchen knife was definitely used.'

Velázquez turned and saw the stocky form of Juan Gómez, approaching. The Inspector Jefe acknowledged him with a nod of the head. 'I'll need you to check and see if this one was shot the same way as Father Pedro, of course, Juan,' Velázquez said. 'And if so, then we'll need Ballistics to run tests to see if the same sort of bullet was used.'

'If I were a betting man,' Gajardo said, 'I'd lay my mother-in-law's undies that it turns out to be the same kind of bullet.'

Gómez looked at Velázquez and jerked his thumb in Gajardo's general direction. 'The way your number two's going, Luis, he'll soon be a very rich man.'

'Either that or his mother-in-law's going to feel the cold a lot more this winter,' Velázquez said.

Gómez set his briefcase down at his feet. 'I don't know what's going on in this city,' he said. 'Priests never use to get brutally murdered.'

'They did back in the Civil War. And often they were castrated first.'

Gómez brought out a packet of Camels, shook one from the pack and lit up.

Velázquez flashed him a sideways look. 'I thought you'd packed up?'

Gómez took a long drag, then exhaled. 'I did.'

'Nothing like will power, is there?'

'So they tell me.'

Velázquez heard someone coming up behind him. He turned and found himself looking at Judge Montero. 'What have we got, Inspector Jefe?'

Velázquez quickly brought him up to speed.

'What do you want me to do now, boss?' Subinspector Gajardo asked.

'Not much you can do here, José.' A quick glance at his watch told Velázquez that it was coming up to 6 a.m. 'If I were you, I'd go home and grab a little kip. See you at the Jefatura first thing in the morning.'

'Okay. *Buenas noches.*'

Velázquez remained at the crime scene for a while, talking to the Médico Forense, before he drove back to the Jefatura. He left the car in the basement car park and went to a bar on Blas Infante that opened early. He had the waiter bring him café con leche in a glass and a croissant.

Ana would say he was parading his working-class roots having his coffee in a glass. Truth was, he just preferred it this way.

He had the waiter bring him a glass of brandy, then poured it into his coffee to make a carajillo.

Ana would tell him off for drinking spirits first thing in the morning, too.

But she didn't know he was hooked on heroin.

And it was better that way. What she didn't know couldn't hurt her.

The brandy, mixed in with his coffee, tasted good and invigorated him.

He paid the bill, then went back to the Jefatura and took the lift up to his office. No sooner had he sat at his desk than his telephone rang. He snatched it up. '*Hola*?'

It was Comisario Alonso wanting to be updated on what Velázquez had managed to turn up so far.

The Inspector Jefe told him what was new.

Gómez looked up from the body laid out on the dissecting table as Velázquez entered the lab first thing the following morning. 'Hi, Luis,' the Médico Forense said. 'You look terrible.'

'Thanks, *amigo*.'

'No, seriously, I mean it. I didn't notice it earlier, because it was dark down by the river, but you look like you haven't slept in a month.'

Velázquez shrugged, thinking Gómez looked pretty knackered, too. 'Is there anything new that you can tell me?'

'I found a bullet.'

'Was it in the same place as with the first victim?'

Gómez nodded. 'You got it in one.'

'I'll need it to be sent to Ballistics for them to compare it with the bullet taken from Father Pedro Mora.'

'It's already been sent over.'

'I can see you've been busy this morning, Juan.'

'You know me, Luis.' The Médico Forense picked up a clipboard and looked at the report that was attached to it. 'The body temperature of the second priest doesn't tell us much, of course, because–'

'The body was found in the river, so it would've been affected by the temperature of the water.'

'Exactly.'

Gómez asked Velázquez whether he'd had any breakfast yet. Velázquez nodded. 'I stopped off in a cafe before I came here.'

'I'm going for mine now.' Gómez hung up his lab coat.

'I'll walk down with you,' Velázquez said, and they went out through the swing doors.

While they waited for the lift, Gómez asked Velázquez how things were going with Ana.

'Just great,' he said.

'You're that rare beast, Luis–a cop who's happily in love.' The doors opened, and they stepped inside. It was empty, and Gómez pushed the button for the ground floor.

The lift began to descend. Velázquez said, 'Ana's just about perfect. She's young and beautiful, honest, loyal, intelligent, and she's a great cook. I really don't know what a woman like her sees in an old guy like me. I mean, she could have anyone she wants.'

'Carry on like that and you'll make me hate you.' Gómez smiled. 'Tell me she's got bad breath.'

Velázquez laughed. 'It's not as though we don't have our ups and downs like any other couple.'

'That's better…tell me more of that stuff. Tell me you argue like hell and scratch each other's eyes out.'

Velázquez laughed. 'You're forgetting something, Juan.'

'What's that?'

'Before anyone starts thinking they ought to feel jealous of someone like me, they ought to remember I'm a guy who's married to a bullfighter.'

'And that's not always easy, huh?'

'You're too damned right it's not,' Velázquez said.

'But you've done it twice, Luis – married a bullfighter, I mean.'

Velázquez shrugged as he thought back on the rather odd direction his emotional and romantic life had taken. His first wife, Pe, had been beautiful, too. She presented a popular breakfast show on television, and everything was just fine for a while. Until one fine day she told him she wanted to pack in her job and become a bullfighter, like her famous father.

Velázquez had been dead against it, as most husbands in his shoes would have been. But Pe hadn't been one to listen to anyone, once she had a bee in her bonnet.

And so his first wife had become a bullfighter. And she was a pretty damned good one, too – at first she was, anyway…until one hot afternoon up in Madrid, she took a goring. They rushed her to the hospital, but she was dead on arrival.

Anyone might have thought that would be enough suffering for any man. And so it proved for the following seventeen long years. During that time, Velázquez had mourned his wife's death. But then one evening he found himself being introduced to a young woman at a party, and something special happened. Call it love at first sight. That woman was Ana, his current wife. She was only twenty-two when they first met, and Velázquez had reckoned she was far too young for him. Either that or he was far too old for her. But somehow they began seeing each other.

Like his first wife, Ana was born into a great bullfighting family, and she made no secret of the fact that she hoped to follow in the footsteps of her father and her uncle, both of whom had been professional *toreros* in their day. Velázquez wondered how it could have happened that he had fallen in love with another female bullfighter. Was there something in his personality that attracted such women to him? Or perhaps he had it the wrong way round: maybe he was drawn to female bullfighters.

But surely that couldn't be true. After all, he had met his first wife well before she told him of her intention of becoming a *matadora*. And had he not done his best to try to talk her out of it?

When he'd first found himself becoming involved with Ana, who was also young and beautiful and obsessed with the idea of fighting bulls, Velázquez put it down to an odd coincidence. Besides, he felt sure at the time that the relationship couldn't last. The age difference between them was just too great, he felt. He supposed theirs was destined to be one of those short, if passionate, flings that burn themselves out before either party has time to consider what exactly they had been getting involved in.

But it didn't turn out that way. Somehow the more he and Ana saw of each other, the deeper their attachment became. And before Velázquez knew it, he was getting married for the second time, some twenty years after he'd married his first wife.

And for better or worse, the day he walked Ana up the aisle she was only a year older than Pe had been when he'd married her.

Velázquez snapped out of his reverie and looked at Gómez. 'All I know for sure, Juan, is that I get sick with fear every time Ana steps into a bullring.' He sighed. 'And I always felt the same way when I was with Pe back in the day.'

The Inspector Jefe headed for home, and checked in on Ana as soon as he got back, to see if she was up yet. And finding that she was still sound asleep, he decided not to wake her. She would need all the rest she could get before the bullfight later in the day. Velázquez took the baggie from its hiding place, and went into the kitchen and shot up. Then he drove back over to the Jefatura. The heroin had given him a second wind, so that instead of feeling exhausted after what had been a sleepless night, he felt strangely high and full of energy.

Serrano and Merino were already at their desks when Velázquez entered the office. He said '*Buenos días,*' then booted up his computer, before he told the two officers there had been a second murder. 'It's another priest,' he said. 'The body was found in the river in the night. The victim served at the same church over on the Plaza de San Lorenzo.'

Jorge Serrano sat up in his chair. 'Do you think it could be a serial killer we're after then?'

'If so, it's one who's got a serious grudge against priests,' said Gajardo, who had just come breezing in. Despite not having slept much, he was looking as spruce and dapper as ever in his summer suit.

Javi Merino said, 'It seems like quite a coincidence that he should've served at the same church as Father Pedro, boss, don't you think?'

Serrano fixed the younger officer with a thoughtful look. 'Or maybe it's not at all.'

'That's exactly what I was thinking.'

Just then, Sara Pérez came into the office. She said good morning to everyone, then went over to Velázquez, who was sitting at his desk. 'I thought you might want to read this, boss,' she said, and handed the Inspector Jefe the previous day's edition of El Sur.

'What is it?'

'This woman author is writing a book about Father Pedro. There's an interview she's given about it in there.'

Velázquez saw the headline: BOOK ABOUT MURDERED PRIEST. He glanced through the article, then looked up at Sara Pérez. 'So the woman's not written the book yet?'

'No, she's working on it now. A journalist friend of mine that works for the newspaper put me wise to her, boss.'

'Have you spoken to the author yet?'

'I called her a few minutes ago.'

'And?'

'She claims to've had an affair with Father Pedro Mora.'

'Would this have been before he became a priest?'

'That's right – way back in nineteen thirty-six, on Tenerife. She claims he wanted to marry her.' Pérez's lips curved up in a wry smile. 'Although the affair would've been platonic I should imagine, given the time.'

'No suggestion of his being gay, then?'

'Not so far as I can make out. Although it's always possible he could've been bisexual, of course. Apparently she's going to write about their affair and why he went into the priesthood.'

'Good work, Sara.'

'There's more, boss. The writer sent a copy of her manuscript – what she's written of it so far–to the journalist that called me. Anyway, my friend's just called and asked me if I'd like her to run off a copy. I'll go over and pick it up now if you'd like to read it?'

'I sure would.'

Chapter 7

Two hours later, Velázquez was sitting at his desk poring over the unfinished manuscript Sara Pérez had procured for him. It seemed, as he glanced through it, to be a fairly run-of-the-mill love story, only set in 1936 and with the Civil War bubbling in the background. Boy Pedro meets girl Lucia. Pedro makes a play, but Lucia cuts him off. Pedro threatens to go and do something desperate… 'I swear, if I can't have you then I'll assassinate somebody. Either that or I'll run away and become a priest.'

Velázquez skipped to the end of the chapter. There was a rather touching episode about the young Lucia Segura…

Ordinarily Father never brought his work home. Even so, I had heard him let slip a few comments to my mother about the possibility of an uprising against the Government in Madrid.

This particular afternoon Father seemed quite distraught when he got back, and disappeared into his study. Mother went in to ask if he needed anything, and happened to leave the door ajar. Well, I was nothing if not curious, as you can imagine, so I loitered outside with my schoolbooks for a moment. Then an idea occurred to me, and I put my books on the floor and got down on my knees. If Mother were to come out of the room of a sudden, I would just gather my books as though I had dropped them and go on my way.

So there I was, outside the room, eavesdropping, when I heard Father say that a terrible thing had happened. General Balmes had been trying out a pistol at the shooting range, when a young man in soldier's uniform burst in, brought out a gun and shot him dead. My father, who had been alone with the General at the time, gave chase, but the lad got away. Father was clearly quite at a loss as to why the young man should have shot the General, or who he was working for—unless perhaps it was for General Franco … "But the truly awful thing is," I heard Father say, 'the assassin was none other than that young Pedro chap who's been courting Lucia…' I heard them agree to keep it from me for my sake. Father said, 'Not a word about any of what I've just told you to a living soul.' 'Quite right, Paco,' Mother assented. 'And we must of course make sure he never comes near her again.'

Moments later, I heard footsteps, and Mother emerged from the room. She was clearly affected by the news, because she passed me without saying a word as I knelt and gathered my books. In fact, I don't think she even noticed I was there.

Needless to say, I never saw Pedro again after that. Years passed and the episode with Pedro came to seem little more than a very minor footnote in my life; and now my memories of Pedro are just that – memories… and rather old and dusty ones at that.

I was nevertheless intrigued when I first read in a history book something that gave me cause to believe Pedro–the silly and hopelessly romantic young fool who had courted me–played a vital role in Spanish history.

You see, General Balmes's 'suicide' gave General Franco the pretext he needed to travel over to Las Palmas, to preside over the funeral. And from there Franco was able to coordinate his Rebel Army's attack on mainland Spain of the following day that kicked off the Civil War. 'I swear, if I can't have you I'll assassinate somebody, or run away and become a priest,' Pedro had said.

In rejecting him as I did, was I somehow responsible for transforming Pedro from lover to murderer?

I suppose the real question is, would the Civil War have been averted had I relented and gone on a date with Pedro that evening? Did millions die simply because I rejected him? Was an entire nation forced to endure decades of misery all because I refused to give myself to a young man who had fallen in love with me?

The next chapter switched to Pedro, and told of how General Franco's troops took the villages of El Real de la Jara, Monesterio and Llerena. It told of how they killed and raped and pillaged in Zafra and Los Lobos de Marmona. Then they came to Almendralejo. There the Fascists took one thousand prisoners, a hundred of them women. And the young Pedro seemed to relish in particular his part in firing upon the villagers, until there was not a single one of them left standing.

Some man of God, Velázquez thought in disgust. And it occurred to him that the episodes he'd been reading about might well have some bearing on Father Pedro's murder...

Velázquez got up and took his jacket from the back of his chair, then slipped it on and made for the door. Seeing he was about to leave, Gajardo asked him if he was going anywhere interesting. 'I'm going to talk to Lucia Segura,' Velazquez said and tapped the manuscript.

'Mind if I come with you?' the Subinspector asked.

'Be my guest.'

They took Velázquez's car, and arrived at the author's home in the Old Quarter, on Pérez Galdos, at just after three. The building was an elegant affair with a white stucco façade and louvered shutters. Lucia Segura buzzed them in and was waiting in the doorway when they stepped out of the lift onto the tiled landing of the third floor.

At a glance, Velázquez reckoned she must be around seventy-five, even though she was rather jazzily dressed in black leggings, pink T-shirt and ballet pumps. '*Buenas tardes*. I'm Inspector Velázquez, Jefe del Grupo de Homicidios,' he said, holding up his ID out for her to see. 'And this is my colleague, Subinspector Gajardo.'

'*Buenas tardes*. How can I help you?'

Close up, Velázquez saw that she'd had a number of facelifts. He also noticed how much makeup she was wearing, and added five years or so to his original estimate regarding her age. 'I'm interested in your manuscript,' he said. 'Would you mind if I asked you one or two questions about it?'

'You'd better come in.' The two men went through the door and found themselves in a large open space that served as the living room. Oil paintings and black-and-white photographs hung on the whitewashed walls. Rugs had been placed over the tiled flooring.

'Please take a seat, gentlemen.' She gestured towards the floral-patterned sofa and sat in one of the matching chairs, over by the window. The sun was streaming in, so that Velázquez had to use his hand as a visor. 'I'm sorry,' Lucia Segura said, 'the sun's a nuisance.' She got up and partially closed one of the shutters. 'That's better.'

Once Lucia Segura had returned to her chair, she gave the Inspector Jefe a thin smile. 'So you wanted to talk about my book. Have you read it?'

'*Si.*' In truth he had speed-read the manuscript, flipping through the pages and only stopping to read the odd passage that he felt might possibly be relevant to the investigation. 'I was just wondering if it's true that you knew Father Pedro Mora when he was younger?'

'Oh yes, absolutely. The Pedro in my story is the one who was murdered, sadly. And I did know him very well, yes.'

'From your manuscript it appears that he was very much in love with you.'

'Yes, he was…which is why I was so sad to hear about what happened to him.'

'Do you believe all that stuff about him killing General Balmes?'

'It's what I heard my father tell my mother, all those years ago. It's also what Pedro – Father Pedro – says in his account, and I certainly have no reason to question it.'

'Yes, I wanted to ask you about that.' Velázquez leaned forward, elbows on knees. 'You say in your manuscript that Father Pedro's account was actually written by him. Is that true?'

'Oh yes, absolutely.'

'Why would he have sent you an account of what he'd been up to like that, do you think?'

'Well, I really have no idea, Inspector.' Lucia Segura shrugged. 'You'd have to ask him that.'

'As you know, I'm not in a position to do that, so I was wondering if I could perhaps pick your brain?'

She shrugged. 'I suppose he sent it to me because he was in love with me when he was young.'

'So it was for old times' sake, then, you think?'

'Something like that, I suppose.'

Lucia Segura got up and took her handbag from the marble-topped coffee table, then rummaged around in it until she found her Marlboros along with a lighter. There was a nervous, jerky quality to her movements. She was a ball of energy, and her limbs were stringy and quite free of fat. She dropped the handbag, a little Dolce and Gabbana number, onto the table, then sat down again. She took a cigarette from the pack and lit up. 'Was there anything else, Inspector Jefe?' She took a long drag on her Marlboro, and squinted at Velázquez through a shifting cloud of silky smoke.

Velázquez glanced at his watch. He'd better hurry up and finish the interview if he was going to make it out to the bullring in time to see the *corrida*. Ana would kill him if he didn't.

'There is one more thing, Señora Segura,' he said. 'I was just wondering if you edited the account that Father Pedro sent you? Or does his account appear verbatim and in its entirety in your manuscript?'

'No, I kept it just as it was.' She took another long drag on her Marlboro. 'I didn't cut or change a single word.'

Velázquez and Gajardo headed back to the Iglesia de Jesús del Gran Poder, with the Inspector Jefe at the wheel. He parked up a side street, then the two men climbed out of the car and walked back to the church and went inside. They didn't have to search long before they found Father Antonio. 'I'm afraid there's been some more bad news,' Velázquez said.

'What's happened?'

'Perhaps you should sit down.'

'Just tell me, will you?'

'Father Aloysius has been murdered.'

The priest looked for a moment as though he might be about to fall over. Velázquez reached out a hand to steady him. 'I'm very sorry, Father.'

There was a dazed expression on Father Antonio's face as he looked at the Inspector Jefe. 'But how did it happen?'

'He was found in the river. Otherwise, it was the same modus operandi as was used on Father Pedro. Which means it's almost certainly the same killer.'

'Have you any idea who did it?'

'Not as yet, which is why I was wondering if you might be able to help me?'

'Help you?'

'Did Father Aloysius have any enemies that you know of?'

'I wouldn't know about that, but I do know that he had a tendency to express ideas and views that many people found controversial, to say the least. It's something he had in common with Father Pedro.'

'They were good friends, I believe?'

The priest nodded. 'And they both held the same view on recent history. They believed that the Vatican had some explaining to do.'

'In supporting the Franco regime, you mean?'

'Exactly…they were liberals, modernizers. They felt that the Catholic Church has made something of a habit of failing to stand up for the interests of ordinary working people when the chips are down.'

'And yet they remained true to the faith?'

'They were in favour of fighting for reform from within the church.'

Gajardo said, 'And what do you think about that, Father Antonio?'

'I could understand why they felt as they did.'

'It must be difficult being a priest when you hold ideas like that, I should've thought?'

'Being a priest is never easy, and nor was it meant to be.'

'Why go to all the trouble, then?' Velázquez asked.

'I can best answer that question with a single word, Inspector Jefe: faith.'

'But you sound as though you agree with Fathers Pedro and Aloysius that the Church was batting on the wrong side back in the Civil War?'

'I believe, as they did, that the Church should stand up for the weak and the downtrodden.'

'And the meek shall inherit the earth, is that it, Father?'

'Exactly.'

'And what about the…errors in the past?'

'I should say we certainly need to face up to them and learn our lesson, so that we don't continue to make the same mistakes.'

'But some priests clearly have continued to err, Father.'

'To err is human, Inspector.' Father Antonio pursed his lips into a smile that failed to make its way up to his eyes. 'Besides, when speaking of the Civil War one needs to take the historical context into consideration. The Church found itself in an untenable position. After all, it could hardly have aligned itself with Stalin's Russia, when Stalin was murdering millions of his own people, now could it? And besides, Stalin had banned organized religion.'

'Why couldn't it have resisted both the fascists and the communists?' Velázquez said. 'Why didn't it stand up for the path of right, which is to say of freedom and liberal democracy?'

'It was felt at the time that liberal democracy had no future in Spain—or indeed in Europe. Remember the Civil War was, in the eyes of many, a dry run for the Second World War. And since the British and the Americans refused to get involved, it was generally believed that we in Spain were faced with a stark choice. It was either one thing or the other.'

'It all seems rather black and white, don't you think?'

'If you'd heard the sermons Fathers Pedro and Aloysius gave, you'd know that is precisely what they felt. Manichean was the word they used for it. What can I say, Inspector?' The priest shrugged. 'You are a Spaniard, so you hardly need me to tell you what we are like as a people. Let's say that history shows we have a tendency to go to extremes. And it seems as though somebody who didn't appreciate what Fathers Pedro and Aloysius had to say was just as willing to go to extremes as they were.'

'You mean you think they could have been murdered because of their political views?'

'It's the only reason I can think of.'

Velázquez said, 'Can you give us any names, Father?'

'Names, Inspector Jefe?'

'Of parishioners who might have borne a grudge against the two priests?'

'I'm sorry but nobody springs to mind.'

'I think I should warn you, Father Antonio, that you need to be on your guard from now on.'

'But what makes you say that, Inspector Jefe?'

'Think about it, Father. The other two priests who served at this church have both been murdered in the same manner.'

Father Antonio's eyes flashed and his purplish lips parted. 'You don't mean to say that—'

'It's a possibility that the killer could come after you next, yes.'

'But my sermons have never been anywhere near as controversial as those of Fathers Pedro and Aloysius, Inspector Jefe.'

'I thought you just said you agreed with their views?'

'I do, yes, but even so…'

Velázquez narrowed his eyes, like he was confused about something. 'I don't quite follow you.'

Father Antonio shrugged. 'I shared their take on what happened in the past, but I disagreed with their decision to talk about their views so openly.'

'And why do you think they did that?'

'They felt, as many people do, that we Spaniards will never be able to move on until we face up to the truth of what happened in our collective past. For that reason, they felt people should talk openly about some of the atrocities that occurred in the Civil War.'

'And you disagreed with them?'

'I think it's sometimes better to let sleeping dogs lie.'

'It's possible that you have nothing to worry about, Father,' Velázquez said. 'But I must warn you that I can't be at all sure of that right now. Nothing is certain.'

'So what are you saying exactly?'

'Use your common sense, and don't take any chances. If someone calls asking you to go to their home, tell them you're too busy. Avoid walking in dark, isolated places on your own at night—car parks, that kind of thing.' Velázquez reached into his pocket and brought out his card. 'And please call me if anything occurs to you, or if anything unusual happens, okay? And I mean anything.'

Chapter 8

'...And that concludes the review of yesterday's bullfights at Las Ventas –'. Velázquez turned the radio off. Moments later, he pulled up outside his flat, hurried inside and shot up in the kitchen. Then he drove back to Forensics, to pick up Juan Gómez, and they headed off for Antequera.

Velázquez's nerves were in tatters by the time they finally arrived at the bullring. A part of him dreaded what he was about to watch. And yet he wouldn't miss it for the world.

They found their seats near the *barrera*, where they would have a perfect view of everything. Gómez produced a small flask from his breast pocket and took a swig. He offered it to Velázquez. 'This might help to calm your nerves a little, Luis.'

'Why? Do I look like I'm nervous?'

Gómez grinned. 'Is the Pope a Catholic?'

Velázquez took a swig of the Scotch. It was a good single malt, and it ran down his throat like liquid fire.

The band started up and then the first bullfighter strutted into the ring, along with his team of peones. Capes windmilled round the bull, teasing and warming him up, then the *picadors* started in.

Velázquez's thoughts returned to the case during the rest of the first and second tercios. He only really began to focus on what was happening in the ring once more during the final suerte, when the young bullfighter went in for the kill. The *matador* stood stock-still. The music started. He lined up his sword. Velazquez thought the lad was rather tall for a bullfighter and cut an ungainly figure. The music stopped. The bullfighter cried '*Toro!*' And again '*Toro!*' – and the beast charged.

The lad ran to meet it, thrust his sword into the animal's neck, and jumped aside in a jerky, uneven movement. The sword went flying through the air and landed some distance away. The lad scampered after it, and only regained his cool when he had the sword back in his hand.

Now Velázquez saw Ana appear below, in the callejon. He watched her as she went and stood behind the *burlador*, from where she could follow the action in the arena.

The bullfighter lined up his sword once more and cried: '*Toro*!' And again: '*Toro*!' The tired animal charged. This time, the bullfighter managed to get the sword to stay in the animal's neck, but the beast refused to go down.

It took him six attempts to kill the bull. The crowd was getting restless by the end, and there were some jeers.

Next it was the turn of Ana and her team. Velázquez's belly turned over as he watched her stroll out into the ring. He didn't want to have to watch what was about to happen, and yet he was unable to turn away. As for Pe, she looked as though she were completely alone with her own thoughts. Velázquez said a quick prayer and crossed himself.

Gómez saw him and followed suit.

The first tercio began. The bull charged one of the horses from the side, hooking up repeatedly with its horns. The horse was wearing armour, and the *picador* jabbed at the bull with his lance and drew blood. Then the *banderillero* made his entrance and the bull switched its attention to him.

The *banderillero* waited until the last moment, before neatly stepping aside and stabbing the animal in the neck with his *banderillas,* to the applause of the crowd. Having done what was expected of him, the *banderillero* sped off and skipped behind the *burlador*.

Ana strutted over to the bull and drew it towards the centre of the ring, then stood, taut and still, her cape stretched out in front of her. The bull looked at her and stamped its hoof. It charged, hooking upward with its horns as it filled the cape, its energy now turning to anger at missing its target.

Next Ana made to execute another media veronica, but midway through she went over the bull's horn and turned her back on the animal as it followed the cape. This brought applause and cries of 'Olé' from the crowd and the band struck up a *pasodoble*, in tribute to Ana's faena.

And Ana carried on like that. Her movements were as easy and supple as a cat's: hypnotic, rhythmic and apparently effortless. Velázquez sat in silence, marvelling at her skill, while the crowd roared out another chorus of olés. The band started up once more. Gómez touched Velázquez on the arm and said, 'This is real bullfighting.'

Velázquez turned fear-wracked eyes on his friend. His only immediate concern was that Ana shouldn't get hurt. The quality of her work was the last thing he cared about, even though he had taken good note of it.

'No, I really mean it,' Gómez said, mistaking the fear and anxiety in Velázquez's expression for disbelief.

Velázquez turned back to watch Ana perform another veronica, followed by a larga cordobesa, a pass which ended with the cape resting on her shoulder. There was another fanfare from the band, then another chorus of olés, followed by more applause. It was clear to Velázquez that the crowd had really warmed to Ana. She had washed away the bad feeling left by the rather inept young *matador* earlier.

The music stopped, only for it to begin again moments later to announce the beginning of the final suerte. The crowd quietened down. Ana lined up her sword and sighted the bull along it. This was the last and most important part of the bullfight. Even though Ana had performed brilliantly up until now, every pass that she made having been executed with unhurried mastery, it would all count for little if she failed to make an effective kill. The vital area in the animal's neck was no bigger than a cien-peseta coin. If you missed the small target but still got the sword in the bull's neck then you might strike bone, and, like the previous *matador*, suffer the indignity of seeing your sword go swirling through the air.

The bull charged and Ana remained stock-still. The beast got closer and closer…and then, just as it seemed she had left it too late and there was no escaping the bull's horns, Ana jumped to the side and rammed her sword into exactly the right place. The bull collapsed headfirst into the sand, blood pouring from its mouth. The small crowd went wild as the band started to play.

No sooner had Velázquez and Ana entered their flat, after driving back from Antequera, than the Inspector Jefe's mobile began to ring. '*Hola?*'

'I've traced your old car, boss–the Alfa Romeo.'

'Excellent work, José. Where was it?'

'Somebody used it in a hit and run attack.'

'They what?'

'The Científicos are still going over it at the moment, to see if they can come up with any DNA or prints,' Gajardo said. 'They told me they'll return it to the impound when they've finished with it. So you should be able to pick it up from there in the morning. And you'll never guess who the victim is–only our friend Ramón Ochoa.'

'*Joder*. Is he okay?'

'He's in the Hospital de la Macarena. The last I heard he was still in a coma.'

'*Cojones*. Have you been in to see him?'

'Not yet.'

Ana said that she was going to take a shower, and Velázquez told her he needed to go out.

'At this hour?' she said. 'Just when I was in a mood to relax and get you to help me celebrate my triumph in the bullring.'

Velázquez shrugged. 'Sorry, but it can't be helped. Something's cropped up.'

'Can't it wait until tomorrow?'

'It's an emergency, Ana,' he said. 'I'll try not to be too late.' Heblew her a kiss as he left the flat, then went and found his car where he'd left it parked, just along from the door to the block. He climbed in behind the wheel and set off down Calle Teodosio, then zigzagged through the narrow streets as far as Calle Feria. He passed the fish market and bars and shops on either side as he headed down to the end, then turned right into Resolana, went past the Macarena Basilica and the old city walls, and swept up past the big building where the Parlamento de Andalucía sat, and the Macarena Hospital was a little way up over on the left. He pulled into the parking area outside, and saw that a posse of reporters and cameramen were standing by the front steps, waiting for him.

Velázquez shat in the milk under his breath, as he hurried over towards the entrance. Then they spotted him, and the next moment he found himself moving slowly through a gauntlet of reporters all barking questions at him. How was the victim? And how was it that Ramón Ochoa had ended up in hospital in the first place?

Velázquez kept saying 'No comment', trying to look impassive. The pack of reporters stuck with him all the way up the steps, but he managed to squeeze in through the glass doors. He hurried over to the peroxide blonde on reception, and told her that he'd come to see Ramón Ochoa.

The woman picked up the phone and asked after Ochoa. She was put on hold for a short time, but then she found herself speaking to someone who knew the situation regarding Ramón Ochoa. After a brief exchange, the woman hung up. Then she told Velázquez that Señor Ochoa was in no state to receive visitors. Velázquez showed the woman his ID and asked if he could speak to the doctor who was treating Ochoa. The woman said she would see what she could do, and picked up the phone once more. She had to go through several people, but she finally got the doctor on the line.

After she had finished speaking, the woman hung up and told Velázquez that Doctor Carmona was on his way.

The doctor duly appeared, minutes later. A man in his late thirties, of medium height and build, with short black hair and a quiet manner, Doctor Carmona told Velázquez that Ramon Ochoa was still in a coma. It was impossible to say what the patient's chances of recovery were.

Velazquez left his number, and asked the doctor to notify him immediately if there was a change in Ochoa's condition. Doctor Carmona promised to do so, and with that Velázquez left the hospital and drove home.

No sooner had the Inspector Jefe climbed out of the car than he was hit by a wave of dizziness and nausea. He needed a fix and knew he'd only get worse until he had one.

Problem was, he had no heroin left.

He needed to go and score or he was screwed.

The best place to score horse was either over on the Alameda de Hercules, or out in the Tres Mil Viviendas. There would be far less chance of being spotted by one of his colleagues out in the Tres Mil.

He was about to get back into his car when he thought better of it. It would be wiser to get a taxi, because you couldn't park anywhere in the Tres Mil without running a serious risk of having your car stolen. He walked the short distance over to the Plaza del Duque, climbed into the back of the first taxi in the rank, and told the driver where he wanted to go.

'I don't go to the Tres Mil,' the driver said. 'You won't get anybody else to take you there, either. Too dangerous, especially at this time of night.'

'Just take me as close to it as you consider safe, then.'

They set off, and after they'd gone some way the driver said, 'D'you live there?'

'No.'

'I didn't think so.' The driver was looking at Velázquez in his mirror. 'You don't seem like the kind of person who'd be living in a place like that, if I might say so. Are you sure you still want to go there?'

'*Sí.*'

'It's just that the place has got a terrible reputation, you know,' the man said. 'Some of the stories I've heard are enough to put me off taking people to that part of town, I know that much.'

'What stories are these, then?'

'They've stopped taxis and made the drivers get out at gunpoint…taken everything from them, including the car. One driver came walking back in his underwear.'

'What about the police, don't they do anything?'

'People reckon the cops are too frightened to go in there, unless they go in large numbers and armed to the teeth,' the cabby said.

When they got to the other side of Bami, the cabby pulled over. 'This is as far as I go.'

Velázquez paid the fare, then got out and started walking. It was dark and there weren't many people about. He passed a bar full of old guys talking over a drink, and pressed on until he eventually found himself at the start of a street lined with rundown blocks of flats. Up ahead, a little group of prostitutes were standing on the corner. They called to Velázquez as he passed. 'How d'you fancy taking a trip to Mars, *hombre*?'

'I thought that's where this is,' Velázquez felt like telling them but didn't.

Turning the next corner, he found himself on a long, broad street. A rubbish container had been tipped over, its contents left sprawling over the pavement. A dog went running past. Then Velázquez came to a bar. There were a number of motorbikes parked outside.

He entered the place, and was immediately struck by the smell of disinfectant and marijuana. Or maría, as the locals called it. The men at the counter turned and stared at him. Some of them were dressed in leathers. The clientele seemed to be made up of a curious mixture of bikers and gypsies. Velázquez acted like he didn't notice all the attention he was getting.

The barman came over and made a show of looking him up and down. The man was an enormous chunk of formless cement with a forest of greasy black beard. 'You new here,' he said. It wasn't a question.

Velázquez said, 'What's the matter, do you only serve regulars?'

'Depends what people come here lookin' for.'

'I need to score a wrap of horse.'

The man looked at him in stony silence for a moment, as did some of the other men at the bar. Velázquez could hear the whir of a propeller fan. 'Wouldn't be a poli, would you?'

'Do I look like one?'

The man shrugged. 'Look like shit, so you could be.'

'Do polis usually come in here saying they need to score heroin?'

'Even polis ain't usually that stupid.'

Chapter 9

'Well,' Velázquez said, 'either you can help me or you can't. Do you know anyone who's selling around here?'

One of the men at the bar took a last drag on his joint, then gestured to Velázquez, before he got off his stool and headed for the toilet. The man had the appearance of your typical biker, down to the greasy ponytail and swastika on his jacket lapel. But that didn't bother Velázquez. Right now the Inspector Jefe was too desperate for a fix to concern himself with such matters.

No sooner had the toilet door slammed shut behind him than Velázquez found himself being shoved back against the wall. It was too dark to see anything, and he felt a cold metal blade against his throat. The biker must have flicked the switch by the door, because the light came on. '*Por cojones*. What the fuck is this?' Velázquez said.

'What do you want here?'

Velázquez began to make out the man's face, as his eyes adjusted to the lack of light. 'I need to score some heroin, like I said. What's with the knife, *hombre*?'

'You better not be a cop.'

'I told you, I need a fix.'

'I heard you…only you look like a cop to me.'

'Just sell me some horse and I'll be on my way.'

The man lowered the knife and took a step backwards. 'I dunno about you, *hombre*. You got something about you…a certain look I don't trust.'

'For fuck's sake, I need a fix I tell you. Look at my forehead. I'm clammy with sweat. I need to score. *Joder*.'

'How much do you want?'

'How much'd four wraps be?'

'Thirty thousand *pesetas*.'

'That's way too steep.'

The man shrugged.

Velázquez figured he didn't have much choice. 'Okay.'

63

The man continued to look at him, like he was trying to make up his mind. Then he said, 'Wait here,' and went out.

Minutes later, the man returned and said, 'Looks like it's your lucky day.' He reached into his pocket and pulled out a baggie. 'Didn't come in wraps this time,' he said. 'You'll have to take it like this.'

Velázquez felt he was being tricked. 'That's less than four wraps.'

'Looks like more to me.' The man shrugged. 'Price is thirty thousand *pesetas*. Take it or leave it.'

Velázquez reached into his pocket and took out the money. The man snatched the banknotes and pocketed them before he handed over the baggie. 'Wait in here a coupla minutes before you come out.'

'Okay, but what's the big deal? Don't get cops down this way, do you?'

'You never know, there might be the odd lone poli sent here undercover to spy on us.'

The man leered at Velázquez again, then he turned and went out. Velázquez wasn't in any great hurry to leave anyway, as it happened. He went into the cubicle and took out the spoon, hypodermic needle and other paraphernalia he carried in his pocket at all times nowadays, then heated the heroin.

He rested his head back against the wall and shut his eyes, then jabbed the needle in and experienced moments of great peace. Moments that were as precious to him as they were injurious to his general well-being and lifestyle in the long term.

He stayed like that for some minutes, enjoying the sensations he was feeling, before he finally left the bathroom and hurried on through the bar and out into the street.

He hurried back the way he'd come, going past the bar he'd seen earlier. There were still a few old boys sitting in there, chatting over a drink. Men with nobody to go home to.

2

TERCIO DE BANDERILLAS.

The matador *waited for the bull until the last fraction of a second. It seemed as though the horn was about to go in, that the matador had left it too late; but then he rammed the sticks in and skipped clear all in one supple movement.*

Chapter 10

Ana was asleep in bed by the time Velázquez got home, but he didn't feel like sleeping yet, so he turned on the television and made himself comfortable on the sofa. He surfed the channels, until he found a news channel that happened at that moment to be broadcasting a report on the murder investigation he was currently running. 'As yet no arrests have been made,' he heard the reporter say. 'Sources close to the police force have revealed that Homicide detectives are running around chasing their own tails in their search for the priests' killer.

'And we can also reveal there has been a curious new development today which appears to be linked in some way to the investigation into the murder of the two priests, after an Alfa Romeo was found abandoned in the aftermath of a hit-and-run incident in which a young Sevillano, Ramón Ochoa, was knocked down and left in a critical state.

'Senor Ochoa is now in hospital, where we understand that he is in a coma. And it appears that the car involved in the incident has been traced to Inspector Jefe Velázquez, the very man who is in charge of running the investigation we have just been speaking about.

'What is more, Inspector Jefe Velázquez is the husband of the *matadora* Ana Velázquez. The couple have been much talked about in the gossip columns recently, usually for quite different reasons; but this is most certainly not the kind of publicity they will welcome.

'And we can reveal that on Wednesday afternoon, Inspector Velázquez was seen chasing Ramón Ochoa from Jorge's, a gay bar in Triana, in front of a barroom full of witnesses.

'The detective also spoke to an Eric Waters, a friend of Ramón's, who teaches at the Escuela de Idiomas.

'According to Waters, Inspector Velázquez was keen to find Ramón and talk to him.

'Now this latest hit-and-run incident that has been traced to the Inspector Velázquez – or to his car, at any rate – has given rise to rumours that what happened to Ramón Ochoa might not have been an accident.'

The next moment Velázquez saw himself on the screen walking up the steps at the front of the Macarena hospital, surrounded by reporters. There was a furious look on his face on the screen, as he kept saying 'No comment' in response to the reporters' questions.

Seeing himself like that made Velázquez think of a bull that is cornered by a *matador* and his *picador* and *banderilleros*. Then, mercifully, his face was gone and the anchor moved onto the next news item.

After watching this latest PR nightmare, Velázquez shat on the forebears of the scumbags whose reports he had just had the misfortune to listen to. But he would be buggered sideways by a bull if he was going to let any of this get to him. Things were bad enough anyway, without his joining in on the side of his oppressors.

Anyway, that was Spain for you, he thought. It's the kind of people we are. We're a nation of folk who're always on the lookout for a bull to stick a *pica* or sword into. And right now, he found himself playing the role of *toro*. Thankfully, he was much too high on heroin to let it really get to him. Screw the bastards.

He left the flat and drove over to the Jefatura to pick up Lucia Segura's manuscript from his desk, where he'd left it, then brought it home with him. Then he stretched out on the sofa and began to read, picking up where he'd left off…

One of my fellow prisoners, a German lad called Klaus, said he wanted out of the war. He planned to escape and asked if I wanted to go with him. But I was convinced that our forces would break through any day, and I longed for them to come and rescue us. Or at least, I did at first – until Klaus, who had been flying with the Condor Legion of the German Luftwaffe that destroyed Guernica, told me how the bombing was authorized by German feldmarschall Wolfram Von Richthofen, and ultimately therefore also by General Franco himself. When I heard that I lost all faith in the Nationalist cause and decided to escape; so when the reinforcements stormed the makeshift camp the following day, I seized my opportunity...

Pedro went on to describe how he came across an injured Anarchist whom he helped back to his people in the mountains. Once there, Pedro was able to pass himself off as a fellow Republican, and worked hard to try to escape his past. And he very nearly succeeded in doing so, Velázquez thought.

But not quite, of course...

Velázquez yawned and glanced at his watch. It was coming up to 3:30 a.m. and his eyelids felt like they were loaded with lead weights. He put the manuscript down, then lay back on the sofa. The next moment he was fast asleep. Only sleep, when it came nowadays, rarely offered him any respite from the thoughts that troubled him during his waking hours, and it was no different on this occasion.

He was sitting in a chair, blindfolded, and the Black Lady was giving him a load of flannel about New Orleans that he didn't believe a word of. He'd be surprised if she'd been further afield than Dos Hermanas, and he told her as much. He asked the woman whom she and her boyfriend were working for. Was it his old nemesis, Diego Blanco, that had got them to do this?

'Now, now,' the man – Bill, as he called himself – said. 'You ought to know better than to ask the Black Lady a darn fool question like that...especially seeing as she's come all this way just for you.'

Then the needle went in.

And then Velázquez woke up.

Feeling clammy and sick, he stumbled out to the bathroom and splashed cold water over his face, then stood looking at himself in the mirror. He took in the unhealthy-looking skin, the wild eyes with their broken veins. He found himself wondering whether they were the eyes of a man who was in his right mind.

Velázquez drove over to the impound to pick up his old car first thing the following morning. He was happy to get his Alfa Romeo back, and he drove in to the Jefatura and worked on his report for an hour.

He had just taken a sip of the liquefied mud Serrano had brought him, courtesy of the machine downstairs, when the telephone on his desk began to ring. '*Diga*?'

'This is Doctor Carmona.'

'*Hola*, Doctor. What's happened? Has there been a change in Ramón Ochoa's condition?'

'Yes, I'm very happy to say that he has rejoined us in the land of the living.'

'That's great news. Can I come over and talk to him now?'

'So long as you keep it short and sweet, Inspector Jefe. I'm sure I don't need to remind you that he's still in the recovery stage.'

'Of course. Thank you.'

They hung up, and Velázquez rose from his chair. Gajardo looked over. 'Off somewhere, boss?'

'Ochoa's come out of the coma.'

'In that case, I'll come with you.'

'No, I'll handle this alone, José. You'd be better employed knocking on more doors round where Father Aloysius lived. Take Javier with you.'

'What about me, boss?' Pérez asked. 'Want me to go with them?'

'Yes, but first you can get onto Ballistics for me, Sara,' Velázquez said. 'See if they can tell us anything yet about the two bullets that were found in the victims. And call me straightaway if they've come up with something.'

Jorge Serrano asked the Inspector if there was anything he needed him to do. Velázquez told him to go over to Jesús del Gran Poder. The Inspector Jefe was working his arms into the sleeves of his jacket. In truth, it was far too hot in Seville at this time of year for him to be wearing anything other than a shirt, but he had to have somewhere to put his heroin and the paraphernalia he needed to have at hand every time he gave himself a fix.

'Try to find out if either of the murdered priests have any siblings, close friends or relations who are still alive,' he said. 'If so, then find out where they live. Go and talk to them, if they are living in or around Seville. And you'll need to show a little tact, Jorge, because they may not take kindly to being asked about the victims' sexuality.'

Velázquez and Serrano went down in the lift together.

Ramón Ochoa was sitting up in bed when Velázquez entered the room at the hospital. The lad was hooked up to a spider's web of tubes, and one of his hands was chained to the iron bed frame. He looked pale and a little dazed, but he was conscious.

Velázquez smiled and said, 'Glad to see you're back with us, Ramón. We were all worried about you for a while back there.'

Ochoa looked terrified and called for the guard.

Seeing his reaction, Velázquez held up his hands and said, 'I haven't come here to do you any harm.'

'I don't believe you,' Ochoa said. 'It was you that drove at me.'

'Why'd I want to kill you?'

'I've no idea.'

'No, and that's because I have no reason to. But there's somebody out there who wants you silenced for good. And whoever it is reckoned it would be a good idea to kill you and frame me for your murder.'

'Why'd they want to do that?'

'That's easy. They wanted me off the case.'

Ramón Ochoa said, 'The only thing I know for sure's that the driver intended to hit me.'

'Did you see who was driving?'

Ochoa shook his head. 'It all happened too quickly,' he said. 'Besides, my memory of it's a bit hazy.'

Velázquez supposed that was only to be expected, seeing that the man had been in a coma. 'How did you know it was my car, then?'

'My mother told me. She was in here earlier, and she told me she heard it on the news.'

'I'm here to help, Ramón. But I need you to tell me what you know if we're going to catch this guy.'

'Help put me away, you mean?'

'Not necessarily,' Velázquez said. 'Not unless you murdered the priests, that is. Did you?'

'No, of course not.' Ochoa looked confused. 'But if you suspected me of being some kind of mad serial killer who goes around killing priests, then why'd you want to help me?'

'For a start, I'm far from convinced that you're the killer,' Velázquez said. 'And secondly, if people are out there trying to kill you then it's my job to make sure they don't. Besides, the fact that they tried to frame me for your murder tells me something doesn't smell right in the state of Denmark.'

'What's Denmark got to do with anything?'

'For Denmark read Seville.'

'*Que?*'

'Forget it, it's not important.'

Ramón moved his right hand and jangled the chain against the iron bed frame. 'If you really want to help me,' he said, 'perhaps you could take off the cuffs.'

'All in good time, Ramón.'

'I don't get it.' Ochoa pulled a face. 'First I'm framed for the murder of Father Pedro. Then Father Aloysius is killed, and it looks like I'm the prime suspect for both of them. But it's all bullshit. Why'd I wanna go bumping off a couple of priests?'

Doctor Carmona entered the room at that moment. 'Inspector Jefe, I'm afraid your time's up,' he said. 'I really must insist that you leave the patient to get some rest now.'

'Okay. Thanks for answering my questions, Ramón. I'll be in touch.' Velázquez left the room with Doctor Carmona.

'Is he going to be okay now, Doc?'

'I should think so.' Doctor Carmona pushed the button to call the lift. 'But I really must stress how important it is that he should be allowed to rest.'

'Of course. Thanks for keeping me informed and letting me see him.'

'Anything I can do to help a fellow professional, Inspector Jefe–just so long as it doesn't harm the patient.'

The doors of the lift opened. Velázquez stepped in and pushed the button for the ground floor. He stared at the numbers above the doors lighting up in red as he descended.

He was starting to feel clammy again. He realized that it wouldn't be long before he needed his next fix.

Chapter 11

Velázquez passed through the glass doors, ran down the steps, and was heading across the car park when a navy-blue BMW came speeding towards him. He held up an arm, but instead of slowing down, the car speeded up. Velázquez began to run, but the car was getting closer.

He dived through the air and landed on the bonnet of a parked Mercedes just as the BMW went hurtling past, its wheels screeching as it turned at the end of the gangway. The windows of the vehicle were tinted, so there was no way of seeing the driver. But he did manage to get a look at the number plate as the vehicle passed out of the car park and joined the main road.

A man ran over as Velázquez got down off the bonnet of the Mercedes. 'I saw that,' the man said. 'The son of the great whore drove straight at you like he tried to hit you.'

'He did try to hit me.'

'*Joder*. Are you okay?'

Velázquez nodded, then took out notepad and pen, and made a note of the number on the BMW.

'That was quite a dive you made there. Sure you haven't hurt yourself?'

'No, I'm fine, but thanks for your concern.'

'D'you want me to call the police for you, or help you into the hospital?'

'No.' Velázquez smiled. 'It's okay. I'm a policeman.'

'Oh, well, if you're sure you don't need any help…' The man went on his way, and Velázquez continued to his car. He climbed in behind the wheel and set off out of the car park. He passed the Parlamento de Andalucía and the Macarena church, where the bullfighters were supposed to pray before a *corrida*, then went up busy Calle Feria.

He pulled over outside a Basque bar. Men were standing outside on the pavement, talking, one or two of them wearing traditional Basque berets. Velázquez hopped out onto the cobbles, locked the doors, and headed off to his left. He crossed a square, passed a small supermarket, walked up a narrow, cobbled street, then took a right, and the clinic was on the next corner. He went in and made an emergency appointment.

The man behind the counter gave him a slip of paper. Velázquez looked at the two numbers written on it: the doctor's room number, and his own number in the queue. He went and found the room. Four other people were sitting in plastic chairs by the door. He sat down to wait.

And while he waited, he began to feel more and more like he needed a fix.

He wondered who had been driving the blue BMW.

Still wondering, he took out his mobile and called Gajardo.

'*Hola*, boss. What's new?'

'Somebody just drove a car at me,' Velázquez said.

'*Por dios.* Are you okay?'

'*Si*, but only because I got lucky.' Velázquez described the attempt on his life. Then he said, 'The good news is, I saw the reg. Have you got a pen and paper handy?'

'Sure. Fire away.'

Velázquez opened his notepad and read out the registration number.

'I'll check it out now, boss, and get back to you as soon as I've got something,' Gajardo said. 'Where are you?'

'I'm grabbing a bite in a bar,' the Inspector Jefe lied.

'I was about to call you, actually.'

'What's happened?'

'Judge Montero made a call to your desk a short while ago, and I took it for you. He wants to know if we've got a case or not.'

'Tell him we're working on it.'

'That's what I said to him, but he didn't sound too impressed. He said we've got twenty-four hours to come up with something, otherwise it's no go.'

'Better get cracking, then, José.'

'Too right, boss. I'll check out that reg for you.'

They hung up. Velázquez's thoughts turned on the sections of Lucia Segura's manuscript that he'd read. Had the young Pedro Mora really assassinated General Balmes? he wondered.

And if so, then was it possible that the priest might have been killed by a member of Balmes's family out to take revenge?

Two arguments against this possible line of inquiry immediately occurred to Velázquez. First, only four people would have known that it was Pedro Mora who killed Balmes (presuming Lucia Segura's account could be trusted). Those were Pedro Mora himself, and Lucia Segura and her parents.

Second, if a member of Balmes's family really had killed Father Mora to take revenge, then why would they have waited all these years in order to take action?

It was always possible that the killer only found out that it was Father Mora fairly recently, though.

It occurred to Velázquez that if somebody in Balmes's family had discovered the identity of the General's assassin, then it must mean one of two things. The first possibility was that more than four people had known about it. In which case Lucia Segura's account could not be trusted totally.

The second possibility was that one of the four people who were party to the secret–either Lucia Segura or one or both of her parents, or Father Pedro Mora himself–must have divulged the identity of the assassin to a third party.

The latter theory struck Velázquez as being highly unlikely.

The lady in the green dress, who had been before Velázquez in the queue, came out through the door. He stood up and went in.

The doctor, fair-haired and bespectacled, smiled and asked Velázquez what she could do for him. He told her he needed a week's supply of methadone. He found his wallet, took out his health card.

Then his mobile began to ring. '*Diga?*'

'Velázquez, it's Comisario Alonso here. There's been another murder…'

Chapter 12

The victim was lying naked on the bed, and a fingerprint expert, wearing custom-made inspection glasses, was sticking pieces of tape to the bed frame, wall and bedside table. Wherever he saw a print, he'd peel the tape off and store it.

There was no sign of a knife having been used on this one, and the victim had been shot in the head. Which could well mean this was the work of a different killer.

The bullet had gone in above the ear, so that much of the skull was destroyed, with blood and bits of flesh and bone splashed over the walls, sheets and pillows. Despite this, the victim's face was relatively untouched. Foreign, thought Velázquez. Possibly Russian.

Judge Cristobal Montero entered the room, followed by Subinspector Gajardo. Both men were dressed in immaculate summer suits. Looking at them was almost enough to make Velázquez feel underdressed in his chinos, polo shirt and creased linen jacket. But he reminded himself he was a real cop investigating a real murder, and not one in some Hollywood flick.

'*Hola*, boss, Judge Montero,' Gajardo said. 'Got here as soon as I could.' He seemed to be out of breath as he looked at the victim lying on the bed.

Judge Montero shook his head and said, 'What a bloody mess.'

'Looks like he was taken by surprise.' Subinspector Gajardo took out a handkerchief and mopped sweat from his brow. 'Might even have been asleep when he was shot, by the look of him.'

Velázquez nodde. 'That's just what I was just thinking.'

'However it happened,' the Judge said, 'we can't have people being killed right left and centre like this, Inspector Jefe. This is Seville, not the Bronx. *Joder.*'

The Judge leered at Velázquez and then stormed off before the Inspector Jefe could think of a reply.

Gajardo turned his head to look at Velázquez. 'Are the Científicos on their way, boss?'

Velázquez nodded as the door opened, and Juan Gómez entered the room. 'Good afternoon, señores,'
he said, as he came over to the bed and set his briefcase down.

'I wouldn't go that far,' Velázquez said.

The Inspector Jefe drove to the Poligono Sur, pulled over and parked in one jerky manoeuvre, then climbed out of the car. His trousers and the back of his shirt were sticking to his skin as he made his way towards the entrance to the club.

The word BLONDES was written up in big bold letters outside, reflecting no doubt its ungentlemanly owner's general preference where the fair sex was concerned. An odd choice for a name, you might think, in a city where blondes were generally thought to be thin on the ground.

Except they weren't, because they came flocking all the way from Eastern Europe to work in dumps like this.

Diego Blanco, the club's proprietor, was known to the police, and to Velázquez in particular. Truth to tell, the Inspector Jefe had spent a good part of the previous ten years trying to nail the gangster on a whole litany of charges; but somehow he'd always failed to do so. The fact remained, though, that little happened in the city's criminal underworld without Blanco knowing about it. Which was why Velázquez had chosen to come and pay a call on the man now.

It was dark in the club and the place seemed to be doing a fairly good trade, despite the fact that it had only just turned noon. Velázquez spotted Diego Blanco sitting on a stool over at the bar, holding court to a bevy of young women. All of the girls had big breasts, which they seemed to be trying to thrust into the gangster's face. Like some competition, Velázquez thought, where the girl who gets to show the most cleavage wins.

Needless to say, there was a wealth of Botox and silicone on show. Not that Diego Blanco seemed to mind. The man was clearly in his element. Look at him, with his gut pressing against his silk shirt, *torero's* ponytail, leather waistcoat unbuttoned. The thick Cuban cigar he had on the go poked out between stubby fingers studded with gold rings so thick they'd serve as knuckle-dusters. The man looked as though he'd gone to a lot of trouble and expense in order to look that tacky.

Velázquez went up to the bar and asked for a large Johnnie, neat. 'Black or red?'

'Black,' Diego Blanco called through the melee. 'And it's on the house.'

Velázquez turned and said, 'I see you've got company, Diego.'

The gangster shrugged as if to say What can you do? Then said, 'To what do I owe the pleasure?'

'Just thought I'd call in for a chat.'

'You always was one to like a chinwag, Inspector Jefe.'

The barman put Velázquez's drink down on the counter. 'Is there somewhere we can talk?'

'Sure.' Diego Blanco waved his hand and said, 'Come on, girls, give me some space to talk business,' and the sea of cleavages parted. The next moment, the two men were sitting alone at the bar.

Velázquez said, 'There's been a spate of murders in the city of late, Diego, in case you hadn't noticed.'

'If you ask me, this city's gettin' worse than fuckin' Chee-ca-go.'

Velázquez nodded. 'Don't suppose you'd know anything about any of it?'

'*Que*?'

'All these murders?'

'No, they're nothing to do with me, Luis.'

'That wasn't my question.' Velázquez sipped his Scotch. 'It's fair to say you normally have a good idea of what's going down in this city.'

'I've got fingers in a number of pies, it's true,' the gangster said. 'But I don't know nothin' about any of these murders, I can tell you that much.'

'This is good Scotch,' Velázquez said.

'Have another.' Diego Blanco gestured to the barman, then pointed to the Inspector Jefe's glass.

'Nice club you've got here, Diego,' Velázquez said. 'Be a shame if I had to call the attention of certain of my colleagues to one or two of the less legal things that tend to happen on the premises from time to time.'

'No need to get like that, is there? I make you welcome and give you Johnnie Blacks on the house and now you're givin' me this shit? You gotta be taking me by the hair, right?'

'I asked you a question, Diego, and I never got an answer.'

'Look,' the gangster said, 'it's the fuckin' Russkies, ain't it. *Joder.*'

'What is?'

'Fuckin' city's been going downhill ever since they set up shop here. Fuckin' bad news, they are.'

'That sounds a little xenophobic, Diego, if I may say so.'

'I ain't got nothin' against our Russian friends. It's just that I don't want the bastards over 'ere, tha's all. I mean what's the matter with fuckin' Russia? Ain't the place big enough for 'em?'

'So it's all down to the Russians?'

'*Si.*'

'That's easy to say, Diego,' Velázquez said. 'But it doesn't tell me much.'

'Look, Luis, instead of pissin' around comin' here, you wanna take a drive over to the new casino that's opened up in Camas.'

'Now why would I want to do that?'

'A front for our Russkie friends, ain't it.'

Velázquez was beginning to wonder if Diego Blanco might have a point. It all seemed to add up. What if this latest killing had been a mafia hit?

The Inspector Jefe slipped down off his stool and said, 'I gotta go.'

'So soon? Aren't you even going to stay and finish your drink?'

'Don't worry – I'll be back.'

The midday sun was doing its worst, but Velázquez drove with the air con off because it made him feel nauseous. He was dripping with sweat by the time he arrived at the new casino Diego Blanco had told him about in Camas.

It was a large white building with an elegant façade, and looked like some ritzy hotel. Beyond you could see the dry hills baking under the molten sun in the distance. The Inspector Jefe slotted his Alfa Romeo into one of the vacant bays in the parking area, then climbed out and made a dash for the shade. He peeled his sweat-soaked polo shirt from his skin as he headed over to the tongue of red carpet that protruded from the entrance.

The doorman, who looked more like Cary Grant than Arnie Schwarzenegger, smiled and welcomed him in, saying, '*Buenas tardes, señor.*' The electronic doors parted and closed behind Velázquez. He passed through a large atrium with a fountain in the middle of it, and went on into the gambling area.

The place was all red plush, leather and rosewood, and appeared to be doing a reasonable trade despite the time of day. Most of the clientele seemed to be Spanish or South American, and there were also a few Chinese. But Velázquez couldn't see anybody who looked Russian. Nor did he hear any Russian accents. Which might not mean a thing. After all, you could own a place without even visiting it.

Noticing a tall elegant blonde woman in a blue trouser suit, who looked like she was there to keep an eye on the tables, he went over and introduced himself. He told the woman he wanted to see the manager. 'Is there a problem?' she asked.

'No, I just need to talk to him.' Velázquez held out his ID. 'Please come with me.'

Velázquez followed the woman back out to the reception area, then waited while she went behind the desk. He watched her pick up a phone and call her boss. She said something into the receiver that Velázquez didn't catch. The next moment she hung up, then she turned to look at the Inspector Jefe. 'He'll be down in a moment, *señor*,' she said, 'if you'd just like to wait.'

Velázquez thanked the woman. She smiled. It was her pleasure.

Moments later, a man in an elegant grey suit came hurrying over. 'Good morning, Inspector uh…'

Velázquez identified himself and held up his ID. The man looked at it. Velázquez said, 'And you are?'

'I'm Carlos Rodriguez, the manager. Is there some problem, Inspector?'

'I wonder if you could give me a few minutes of your time?'

'Certainly…please come this way.'

Velázquez followed the man up across the atrium and up a few steps and along a red-plush-lined corridor. They went through a panelled door at the end into a room full of TV screens. Rodriguez sat behind the large rosewood desk, and Velázquez sat facing him.

Rodriguez fiddled with the knot on his burgundy tie. 'So how can I help you?'

'Can you tell me who the main shareholders are for this place?'

'A company by the name of Waterford Incorporated owns the lion's share.'

'How much would that lion's share be?'

'Ninety-five percent, to be precise.'

'And where is Waterford Incorporated based?'

'New York.'

'Can you tell me anything else about them?'

Rodriguez shrugged. 'Not really,' he said. 'I'm only the manager of this place. There's nothing in my job description that says I need to know anything about the shareholders' business interests.' He ran a finger over his walrus moustache. 'I'm just here to ensure everything runs efficiently on a day-to-day basis. I manage the staff and make sure they're doing their jobs properly. That includes checking that nobody's on the take and that none of the punters are cheating, either.'

'It's not owned by Russians, then?'

Rodriguez's dark brows rose. 'Russians? Not to the best of my knowledge. Waterford Incorporated doesn't have much of a Russian ring to it, does it? And they're based in New York, as I told you. So no, I can't see it being a Russian company, can you?'

'But you don't know for sure?'

Rodriguez smiled. 'Like I say, knowing stuff like that's not in my remit.'

Velázquez thanked the man for his time and left. The heat hit him as he stepped out of the air-conditioned building. He found his car where he'd left it and climbed in. The wheel was too hot to touch. He buzzed the windows down and gasped to get some air into his lungs.

Once he was able to breathe normally again, he began to consider his next move. Then he started the engine up and headed back into the city.

A big man with a salt-and-pepper beard and bulging headland of gut that protruded over his belt, Jaime Arrese seemed happy to see Velázquez, as ever. 'Neither of us are getting any fitter Jaime,' Velázquez said. 'What happened to your plans to start going to the gym?'

'Why do we always agree to start a new health regime when we're out together in some bar in the early hours with a bellyful of gin in us?'

'Probably,' Velázquez said, 'because we're out in some bar in the early hours with a bellyful of gin in us.'

Jaime laughed and slumped in his chair, behind a desk crowded with piles of folders, a second desk at right angles to it playing home to his computer. Overhead a propeller fan was fighting a losing battle against the incessant heat. He gestured towards the vacant chair and Velázquez sat at on it, then said, 'I hope I'm not disturbing you?'

'You're keeping me from my work,' Jaime said. 'But you're not disturbing me. It's rather a relief to have an excuse to come up for a few minutes from under this mountain of paper.'

Jaime always said this, even though he was in actual fact one of the most hard-working and successful notaries in all Seville.

'Work,' Velázquez said. 'We can't stand doing it, but we can't leave it alone.'

'Rather like women…' Jaime waved his hand as if to say they would save that conversation for their next drinking bout. 'So how can I help you?'

'I need to find out who owns a company that goes under the name of Waterford Incorporated. They have a controlling interest in the new casino that's opened over in Camas.'

'I can look into it for you,' Jaime said. 'When do you need to know by?'

'Is tomorrow too soon?'

'Shouldn't be.'

'Great.' Velázquez got to his feet. 'I'll treat you to lunch at the Rinconcillo at two, then.'

Velázquez was driving along a narrow cobbled street in the Old Quarter, when his mobile began to ring. He answered it, taking one hand off the wheel.

'Boss? It's me,' came Gajardo's voice. 'We've got an ID for the latest victim. Looks like you hit the nail on the head – the man's name was Vladimir Vorosky. The Científicos've finished examining the crime scene, and a passport for the victim was found there. It could be the work of the Russian mafia, after all.'

'We still need proof of that, of course.'

'Assuming you're right and it's a turf war, then the killer's either gotta be another Russian, or – '

'The local competition.'

'Diego Blanco's the first name that springs to mind, boss.'

'Yes, well you can't lift a stone in this city without finding evidence of his influence under it, I know. But even so, we don't want to jump the gun, José,' Velázquez said. 'Matter of keeping on doing the legwork and seeing what we can turn up. Have you checked yet to see if this Vorosky character had any form?'

'Yes, I have. And no, he didn't.'

'Manage to find out how long he'd been in Seville?'

'He moved into his current address back in March.'

'Any idea where he was before that?'

'Afraid not.'

'Did he have an ID number?'

'No.'

'If he came over from Russia in March, then for all we know he could be wanted by the police over there.'

'So what d'you want me to do, boss?'

'Have you got the man's passport with you?'

'Sí.'

'Take a look inside and see where he was born,' Velázquez said.

'Hang on a sec.'

Velázquez listened to Gajardo breathing down the line, then the Subinspector said, 'In Moscow, boss.'

'Date of birth?'

'Tenth of October nineteen seventy-three.'

'Right, well, there's a fair bit to go on, José. Why don't you try and call the cops in Moscow and see if they've ever heard of him. Get someone to make the call for you who can speak Russkie.'

'Where am I going to find a Russian speaker?'

'Use your initiative, José,' Velázquez said. 'Speak to some colleagues, find out the last time somebody had call to use a translator or interpreter. Failing that, try the university. Or else if you really can't find anyone, get Sara to make the call. She speaks pretty good English. It generally serves as a lingua franca.'

'Okay, boss.'

'And if it turns out the cops in Moscow are familiar with this Vladimir Vorosky, then we'll need to know what he was doing over there and who his associates were.'

'Because the chances are some of them are over here now, you're thinking, right?'

'Exactly. I've been making enquiries concerning the new casino over in Camas. I've had a tip-off that it's owned by the Russians.'

'As in the Russian mafia, you mean?'

'Well it's not el puto Bolshoi Ballet I had in mind, José.'

By the time Velazquez entered the lab, Gómez was already at the dissecting table, cutting up the latest murder victim.

'Got anything for me yet, Juan?'

'There are traces of residue in the victim's hair that suggest a different gun from the one used on the two priests.'

The Inspector Jefe made to leave, but Gómez called after him: 'Hey, Luis?'

Velázquez stopped and turned. '*Que*?'

'I've been thinking,' the Médico Forense said. 'You should stop worrying so much about Ana being a *torera*.'

'Huh?'

'She's a natural,' Gómez said. 'And whenever anyone's that good at something, there's only one thing you can do.'

'And what's that?'

'Just let them carry on doing it and wish them well.'

Velázquez called his team together for a briefing at the Jefatura at two thirty that afternoon.

'Okay, so we've now got three bodies.' He turned to the whiteboard behind him and pointed to the victims' mug shots. 'The same modus operandi was used on both priests, and the same kind of bullet,' he said. 'Which suggests of course that the same gun was most likely used in both killings – very possibly a .38 Smith & Wesson.'

'There was a different MO for the Russian, though, boss,' Jorge Serrano said.

Velázquez nodded. 'Absolutely. And traces of FDR were found in Vladimir Vorosky's hair that suggest a different firearm was used on him.'

'So are we saying we're after two killers, or what?' Gajardo asked.

'Could well be.'

'Or it could be the same killer using a different MO to make us fall into the trap of thinking that,' Sara Pérez said.

'That's true, too.' Velázquez gave his chin a thoughtful scratch. 'Okay, so where do we go from here? Anyone got any ideas they'd like to contribute?'

Silence.

'Let's go over what we've managed to learn so far again, shall we?' Velázquez said. 'Who's going to help me out?'

More silence.

'You've been quiet today, Jorge. Perhaps you can tell us something?'

Agente Serrano's blue eyes narrowed. 'Tell you what exactly, boss?'

'Just recap for us what we've learned so far, to help us focus our thoughts. Maybe that way we'll be able to see a line of inquiry we've overlooked.'

'Both priests served at the same church, for one – the Iglesia de Jesús del Gran Poder. First victim called an escort agency and asked them to send a rent boy over –'

'Who's just come out of a coma,' Javier Merino said, 'After an attempt was made on his life.'

'Using my car, which appears to have been stolen with that purpose in mind,' Velázquez said.

Sara Pérez clicked her fingers. 'So Ochoa's the fall guy. He was set up.'

'Exactly.'

'Who by? is the question,' Jorge Serrano said.

'Have we warned Father Antonio that he could be next?' Pérez wanted to know.

Velázquez nodded. 'I've spoken to him about the need to take every precaution.'

'What do we know about this last victim, boss,' Pérez asked, 'other than what you've just told us?'

'Maybe the Subinspector can help us there...' Velázquez turned his head to look at Gajardo. 'Have you managed to talk to any detectives over in Moscow yet, José?'

'I made contact with them a short time ago, boss.'

'Have you got anything to tell us?'

'The detective I spoke to said he'd never heard of a Vladimir Vorosky.'

'The passport could have been fake.'

'That did occur to me, so I faxed a copy over to Moscow. But the face didn't ring any bells there, either.'

'Which doesn't necessarily mean he wasn't mixed up in something over in Russia, of course.' Velázquez scratched his nose. 'Anyway, the rest of you may be interested to know there's a casino that's recently opened out in Camas, and I've had a tip-off that the Russian mafia has a large stake in it. Which seems likely, given that we know the Russians have gained a foothold in the city's criminal underworld in recent times.'

'Maybe this could've been a hit then, boss,' Javi Merino said. 'Is that what you're saying?'

Pérez nodded in agreement. 'Maybe it's all to do with an internal power battle of some kind. You know what these gangster types are like.'

'No, not really,' Serrano said. 'What are they like?'

Velázquez said, 'Yes, perhaps you'd care to enlighten us as to their psychology, Sara?'

Pérez shrugged. 'They've all got dicks bigger than their brains, and egos bigger than both.'

Serrano said, 'Regarding the in-depth knowledge you appear to have acquired concerning the genitalia of certain sections of the community, Sara, are we to understand you've been burning the midnight oil doing special research into this particular area? And if so, have you put your findings in a report so that the rest of us can read it?'

Pérez threw her pen at Serrano, who ducked just in time so that it hit Merino, who didn't, bang on the nose. Merino asked Pérez what he'd done to deserve such treatment. He was lucky the pen hadn't got him in the eye. Pérez apologized and said it wasn't him the pen had been aimed at but the dickhead or capullo with the ginger hair. Serrano offered a beaming smile in reply, like he was finding all this most amusing. And having witnessed this little scene, Velázquez said, 'Children, please, do I have to remind you that we've got a dangerous killer on the loose and it's down to us to catch him?'

Velázquez went out with his team, and didn't clock off until just after 2 a.m. By that time, he was feeling tired and in need of a fix.

So badly in need of one, in fact, that he drove at nearly double the speed limit most of the way back across town. He pulled up with a great screech of rubber outside of the block where he lived, on Calle Teodosio, then dashed into the building, his shoes slipping on the tiles as he hurried through the lobby and on up the stairs to the flat.

There was no sign of Ana in the living room or kitchen, so he looked in the bedroom – and found her in there fast asleep. He went into the bathroom and injected himself with methadone.

It didn't give you the same kind of hit that you got from the real thing. It was less a wild bull charging through your veins than a playful pony. But at least it took away the feeling of nausea and the clammy, fluey sensation.

And it was a step in the right direction: the first step towards kicking the habit altogether.

Fingers crossed...

Chapter 13

The following morning, Velazquez stood looking out his office window while he drank the muck the coffee the machine downstairs turned out. The city's many church spires punctuated the skyline like so many notes on a musical score. It was a score whose dominant chord was the Giralda, which glowed like a jewelled challis away in the distance.

It was just the sort of view you would want to be able to look out on from your office window. And anybody who had been watching Velázquez would no doubt have presumed he was taking a minute or two out to appreciate the visual delights that Seville had to offer. But truth to be told, the Inspector Jefe was far too taken up with the investigation even to notice what was spread out right before his eyes.

He tossed the empty plastic cup he'd been drinking from into a rubbish bin, and then went and sat behind his desk, where he spent the next hour or so writing up his report. Merino and Serrano were doing likewise, and they both made it obvious how much they hated doing it. After hearing the pair of them shitting in the milk for about the fiftieth time within the space of just a few minutes, Velázquez told them, in an accent that was about as Sevillano as the Torre de Oro, to stop touching his balls or *cojones*. Report writing might be dull but it had to be done. Their trouble was, he told them, they were 'of the movies.' He went on to elaborate by pointing out that he knew very well el Dirty jodido Harry and el puto Mel Gibson didn't do a lot of report writing in their films, but what Merino and Serrano needed to realize was that the lion's share of police work in the jodido real world was concerned with collecting and processing data and then reporting upon it so as to make such information freely available for one's colleagues in a comprehensible and assimilable form. Velázquez shat in the milk, before asking whether he'd made himself clear.

Merino and Serrano told him that he had. Perfectly.

89

Velázquez said in that case maybe the pair of them could stop touching his balls or *cojones* and get on with writing their fucking or jodido reports.

As for Gajardo and Pérez, they'd both been working away at their desks in silence all the while, knowing better than to complain. Velázquez was a good boss to work for, but you had to be careful not to touch his balls or *cojones*, particularly when he had the hump or bad milk.

Jaime Arrese was already there, standing at the horseshoe-shaped bar, when Velázquez showed at the Rinconcillo that afternoon. Fat and yet elegant as ever, with his smart pinstriped suit and burgundy tie, the Inspector Jefe's friend hadn't changed much these past few years. Not unless you counted the well-trimmed beard he'd grown.

Behind him pigs' legs hung from hooks above the wooden counter, and the day's menu was chalked up on a blackboard. And, never one to waste time when there was good food on offer, Jaime had already demolished a variety of tapas. He grinned at Velázquez and they shook hands.

'You know something, Luis,' Jaime said. 'The owners of Waterford Incorporated are Russian. Fancy that.'

'Can't say I'm surprised.'

'It's what you were expecting?'

Velázquez nodded. 'I'd had a tip-off that the Russians owned it, and I just wanted to find out whether it was right or not.' He caught the attention of one of the waiters and ordered a glass of Rioja. 'Thanks for finding out for me, and at such short notice.'

Jaime took one of the boquerones from the small dish at his elbow and popped it into his mouth. 'These are good, I must say.' He had a gourmand's appetite to match his girth.

The waiter set Velázquez's glass of wine down on the wooden counter, and he ordered a serving of albondigas and a dish of olives to go with it.

'What's all this about the Russians anyway?' Jaime asked.

'They've been making their presence felt to an increasing degree in the city's criminal underworld.'

The waiter came and set the two dishes Velázquez had ordered down in front of him on the wooden counter, and the Inspector Jefe popped a meatball into his mouth. It was hot and tasted good. He washed it down with a mouthful of Rioja and changed the subject. 'How's Monica?'

'Truth is, the marriage is on the rocks, Luis.'

'No.'

'It's all my own fault for being such an idiot.' Jaime let out a sigh of breathy lament. 'She caught me cheating with my secretary.'

'*Joder.*'

'My father made a lifelong habit of it.' Jaime took a sip of his ribera. 'The way it was back then. Old boy went at it like a bull from what I gather, but Mother never kicked up a fuss.'

Maybe she should have, Velázquez thought. And said, 'I suppose it was different in those days.'

'You're too bloody right it was, Luis.'

'So how bad is it?'

Jaime shot Velázquez a pained look. 'Monica's saying she wants a divorce.'

'Can't you try and make it up to her?'

'I've been pulling out all the stops, but none of it seems to be working.'

Velázquez demolished another meatball. 'I'm truly sorry to hear that, Jaime. I dunno what to say.'

'Nothing to say.' Jaime shrugged. 'The thing about these sorts of situations is, they can go either way, you know?'

Velázquez had gone out with Monica once, and she'd told him she didn't want to marry a cop. Actually he hadn't been looking for a wife at that time anyway, but he never mentioned this since she didn't ask for his thoughts on the subject. The next time he saw her, she was seeing Jaime.

Velázquez's mobile rang. He worked it up out of his pocket. '*Hola?*'

'It's me, boss.' The Inspector Jefe recognized Gajardo's voice with its heavy Sevillan accent. 'I've traced the reg of the vehicle that drove at you to a car which was stolen two days ago over in Bami.'

'Good work, José.' Velázquez sipped his wine, 'Any more news?'

'There's this guy walked into the station yesterday and made a complaint about a brothel out in Camas.'

'Camas, huh?'

'What I was thinking, boss…what with you mentioning the casino over there.'

'Go on.'

'Seems it's run by Russians – the brothel, I mean. Girls are kept in rooms over there, the bloke reckons, and not allowed out.'

'What's the guy's interest in it?'

'He's in love with one of the girls there…wants her to leave and set up house with him.'

'Does the girl want to leave with him?'

'Sounds like she's scared,' Gajardo said. 'She says the Russian who runs the brothel would have both of them killed. But the guy's willing to take the risk.'

'And wants us to help him get her out?'

'Or shut the place down.'

'Sounds like he's got some *cojones*.'

'Have to give him that, boss. I'm not so sure whether he's got much up top, though.'

'Have you spoken to him yet?'

'No, I got all this from the officer he made the complaint to.'

'Torres?'

'That's the man.'

Velázquez chewed on what Gajardo had just told him for a moment.

'Do you want me to go over to the brothel, boss?'

'And do what?'

'That's what I'm wondering.'

'When you build a house it's best not to start with the roof, José,' Velázquez said. 'You don't want to end up getting the guy killed. And the girl would probably take a beating or worse, too.'

'There is that risk, I suppose.'

'Find the guy who made the complaint and bring him in for questioning.'

'I don't have a name or address for him, I'm afraid.'

'How on earth did that come about?'

'The man said his piece to the desk sergeant then left when he was asked for his details.'

'That's a great help.'

'Sorry, boss.'

'Not your fault, José.'

'So what do you want me to do?'

'We need to find this Russian guy, José,' Velázquez said. 'Get Torres to work with the police artist to produce a portrait. We'll get a photo fit made up.'

Velázquez arrived at the Jefatura, some forty minutes later. His office had been turned into an artist's studio. Sketchpads, pencils, ink, and charcoal were all over the place. Torres the desk sergeant was standing over the police artist, looking strained. The artist was sketching feverishly. Torres leaned over him to get a closer look. 'No, his eyes were a little closer together.'

Velazquez glanced down at the sketch as he strolled past them on his way to his desk. A face was slowly taking shape.

'His forehead wasn't so broad,' said Torres.

The artist rubbed out the bits that were wrong. Torres grimaced. 'His ears were bigger, too.'

Gajardo came in, carrying a cup of coffee from the machine downstairs. 'Would've got you one if I'd known you were here, boss,' the Subinspector said. 'Comisario Alonso was looking for you a short time ago. He told me to ask you to go and see him in his office as soon as you arrive.'

'I'd better go and see what he wants, I suppose.'

Torres said, 'His chin stuck out a little more,' as Velazquez made his way out.

The Inspector Jefe went up the stairs and knocked on Comisario Alonso's door.

'Come,' boomed the Comisario's voice. Velázquez entered to find him standing over by the window. A shortish man with plenty of belly, the Comisario's physique resembled an enormous egg. And one look at his face was enough to tell Velázquez he had the bad milk. 'Inspector Jefe,' the Comisario said, 'what in hell's name has been going on?'

'Comisario?'

'Three men have been murdered and a fourth is in hospital after being hit by an Alfa Romeo Nuova Giulietta. And it seems it wasn't any old Alfa Romeo Nuova Guilietta, either, Inspector, but yours.'

'I know, but I can explain – '

'I haven't finished, Velázquez. I've just been talking to a distraught mother who wants to have you charged with attempted murder – or murder one if her son ends up dying.'

'But Comisario – '

'You're off the case – '

'But haven't you heard the news, Chief – Ramón Ochoa's recovered consciousness, and he knows it wasn't me that tried to kill him.'

The Comisario's brows bunched in a slippery frown, as he took on board what he'd just been told. Then he looked at Velázquez and said, 'Has he any idea who did?'

'No, but whoever it was, he tried to frame me.'

'Why would anyone want to do that, Inspector Jefe?'

'Simple, Comisario,' Velázquez said. 'To try and get me taken off the case. The killer tried to frame Ramón Ochoa for killing the two priests, and then he tried to frame me for killing Ochoa. That way the killer must've thought he'd get away scot-free. Case closed, end of story.'

'So you still think it's just the one killer we're after, do you?'

'So far as the two priests are concerned, yes.'

'What about the Russian?'

'We're still trying to find out whether there's a link.'

'Have you got any leads?'

'A number of them, as it happens, Chief.'

The Comisario fixed Velázquez with his stony, unimpressed look. 'So you haven't just been running around in circles on this one, then?'

'Not at all.'

'That's funny, I'd rather picked up the impression you were chasing your own tail and getting nowhere fast.'

'Far from it, we've been making progress on a couple of lines of inquiry.'

'So you will be making an arrest soon – is that what you're telling me?'

'It's only a matter of time.'

'Time's the thing we're running out of fast, Inspector Jefe. Do I make myself clear?'

'We've all been working round the clock on this one.'

Comisario Alonso scratched his bald head. 'Okay,' he said 'I'll give you one more chance, Velázquez. But you'd better make sure you don't screw up this time. Do you hear me? Because if you do, I'll have your ass in the proverbial sling.'

'Thanks, Chief. I won't screw up.'

'I hope not for your sake. It's your career that's on the line.'

Velázquez felt like telling his son of the great whore of a boss to take his proverbial sling and shove it up his proverbial ass, but somehow he managed to hold his tongue.

As soon as the portrait was finished, the Inspector Jefe had a number of photocopies run off. He pinned a few up in the office and around the building, then sent a copy off to the tekkies so they could make a photo fit. He told them it was urgent, and they had it ready before he assembled his team in the office for another briefing at nine the following morning.

He kicked off by saying, 'A Russian's come into the Jefatura complaining that his girlfriend is being held captive in a brothel in Cama. He claims she's forced to work there against her will.' Velázquez handed out the photocopies. 'The picture I've just given you all is a close likeness, according to Torres. So you can take it out with you and show it to people. We need to find this guy and bring him in for questioning.'

'What for exactly, boss?' Agente Serrano wanted to know. 'I mean, what's his connection with the murders?'

'Maybe there is no direct connection,' Velázquez said. 'I've discovered that the Russian mafia owns the new casino over in Camas, and I've had a tip-off that they own the well as the brothel or *puticlub* as well. What's more, my source also seems to think that Vladimir Vorosky had links to the Russian mafia. And although we have no evidence to back this theory up at present, it does seem like a reasonable one – or certainly one that's worth investigating. So if we can find the girlfriend of this other Russian who spoke to Torres, and get her out of the *puticlub*, then she might be able to offer us information about her Russian employers that we could use to make things difficult for them. We might even be able to get the *puticlub* closed down.'

Gajardo said, 'How's this gonna help us get closer to finding out who killed Vorosky, though?'

'These organizations work like a chain. The men at the top get the people at the bottom to do their dirty work for them.'

'That's how they stop us from getting at them,' Serrano said. 'But their system isn't foolproof. No system ever is. Look at the way the FBI closed down the Five Families over in America. And how did they do it? Quite simple, really. They got dirt on people lower down the chain, then gave them a simple choice: either talk or go away for a long time.'

'And they all started talking,' Sara Pérez said. 'Or enough of them did for the FBI to be able to bring down the Five Families, anyway. I read about it.'

'Exactly.' Velázquez nodded. 'So if we can talk to this man and perhaps make contact with his girlfriend, and get her out of the brothel, then she may be able to tell us something that we can use. Because she'll be scared, remember, so we'll be in a position to be able to offer help and protection – for her and her boyfriend.'

'You're hoping she might be able to give us some dirt on one or two of the links in the chain, boss, you're saying, right?' Gajardo said. 'And then if we can charge a couple of guys, we'll be in a position to offer them a deal – '

'They tell us who killed Vorosky,' Pérez said, 'and they get a reduced sentence.'

'Exactly. It's worth a shot, anyway.'.

'But where are we going to start looking for this man whose girlfriend's in the brothel, boss?' Serrano wanted to know. 'He could be anywhere in the city.'

'He's a Russian who speaks pidgin Spanish, so the chances are he's taking lessons.'

'You're thinking language schools, right?'

'It's a good place to start. Talk to the teachers or the people who run the schools. And talk to any Russian students – and Russians in general – you can find as well. If you show enough people the man's portrait, someone out there's gotta know where we can find him. Okay? Any questions? No? Good, so let's get our booties out there and see what we can find.'

Velázquez put his jacket on and took the lift down to the car park with Pérez and Gajardo. 'Ana's got another *corrida*,' the Inspector Jefe said, 'so I wonder if you'd cover for me again, José?'

'Of course, boss.'

'Just a matter of keeping in touch with the others and making sure they all know what they're supposed to be doing. You can contact me on my mobile if you need to, or if any of you find the man we're looking for.'

Velázquez parted from the other two officers in the underground car park, then drove over to the Escuela de Idiomas on Avenida Dr. Fedriani. He flashed his ID at the receptionist, and showed her the portrait of the man he was looking for. She shook her head. 'Sorry, I've never seen him in here.'

'He's Russian.'

'We do have a couple of Russian students. You could always try talking to them.'

'Are they in the school at the moment?'

'No, they come in tomorrow.'

'You got their phone numbers and addresses?'

'Yes, I'll just look them up a moment.'

The woman tapped at the keys on her computer, then found pen and paper. 'Here they are.' Velázquez thanked her, and looked at what she had written as he walked back to his car.

Before starting the engine up, he called Gajardo and passed the names, numbers and addresses on to him. 'Talk to them and see what you can find out, José.'

'Okay, boss. And please send Ana my regards. I hope she gets some good bulls this evening.'

'I hope so, too.'

More than anything, though, Velázquez just hoped and prayed that she'd get through the evening unscathed.

Chapter 14

As he got closer to Torremolinos, Velázquez began to get more and more nervous. Sweat beaded on his forehead. It formed battalions that marched on his eyebrows and down the bridge of his nose, then began to drip onto his philtrum.

What if Ana doesn't come home with me tonight? he thought.

What if the bull ends up winning this time?

Of course the poor beast was destined to lose whatever the outcome…but what if it took Ana with him?

Velázquez felt himself breathing the dangerous air of high anxiety as he pulled up outside of the bullring. He had time for a quick drink to settle his nerves before the *corrida* started, so he entered a bar and had the barman serve him with a large Scotch on the rocks. But the Scotch only made him sweat all the more. He washed it down with a glass of water, then had the barman uncork a bottle of Rioja for him to take.

He showed the man at the gate his complimentary ticket and went and took his seat by the *barrera*, where he had a bird's-eye view. The sun was beating down with all the spite of some particularly vicious Grand Inquisitor, and Velázquez put the bottle to his lips and had a swig. It tasted good.

The trumpets started up, and Ana strolled out into the bullring. Velázquez felt his stomach turn over. At least driving down here, he'd needed to be in control of his car, and that had given him something to think about. But now that he was reduced to playing the role of passive spectator, he was a mass of jangling nerves.

He swigged the Rioja and mopped his forehead with his handkerchief, as Ana and her peones went to work. Then he felt a hand grip him in the belly and twist, and was forced to get up and make a dash up the steps and out into the concourse, in search of the gents'.

He passed a difficult few minutes in one of the cubicles there, but was feeling a little more human by the time he emerged. He washed his hands, poured cold water over his head, and was just enjoying the feel of the water running down the back of his scalp, and over his face, when he heard loud cries coming from outside.

Something had happened.

His heart hammered out a nasty punk-rock beat as he hurried back into the stand. By now the crowd was on its feet, and... Oh my God, no! Ana was being carried from the ring. Her head had fallen to the side, and she appeared to be unconscious.

Velázquez ran down the steps, then climbed up onto the *barrera* and jumped down into the callejon. A man ran over to him. 'You cannot stay here, *señor*.'

'I'm Ana 's husband,' he said.

'Okay, come with me.'

Velázquez followed the man around the side of the ring, and into the infirmary, where a doctor was already attending to Ana. Her tunic was soaked with blood.

Velázquez rushed to her side and the doctor gave him a sharp look. 'I'm her husband,' Velázquez said. Then he took Ana's hand in his and gave it a tender squeeze.

'It's all right, Ana,' he told her. 'You're gonna be okay.' He had no idea whether this was true – not that she would have heard a word he'd said anyway, because she was clearly out cold. He could see from the amount of blood she'd lost that the wound must be serious.

The doctor said, 'She needs to go to hospital – there's no time to lose.'

Tears rushed to Velázquez's eyes as the ambulance men came in and carried her off on a stretcher. I knew this was going to happen sooner or later, he thought. It had always been just a matter of time.

Right from the start, it had always been nothing more than that: just a matter of time.

This thought was terrible to him. The weight of its predetermined fixity, of its uncompromising and merciless déjà vu, hit Velázquez like a truck.

His legs had turned to jelly.

He shat in the milk.

He prayed.

He shat on the forebears of the bull that had gored Ana, even though he knew none of it was really the poor animal's fault, because the *toro* was just a victim in all this.

He prayed again.

He told God He'd better pull out all of the stops to help Ana or else would never pray to Him again.

He assured God that he was expecting to see some evidence on this one, to prove He was really Up There.

He told Him that should such evidence fail to be forthcoming, he would never believe in Him again.

He remembered the thought that had crossed his mind earlier, as he'd driven down from Seville: what if Ana doesn't come home with me tonight?

He remembered the day up in Madrid that his first wife, Pe, had been killed.

He prayed to God that Ana wouldn't now be about to leave him, too.

He began to pray once more.

He figured he should try not to threaten God, if it was divine intervention he was asking for, so he tried a different approach.

In his prayers he began to reason with God.

It wouldn't be fair, he explained to God, for a man to lose two wives in the same way.

Two wives who were still young and beautiful and had everything to live for.

That would be just too much.

Not only that, but it would be unjust.

The stretcher-bearers disappeared with Ana into the back of the ambulance. Velázquez went to climb in the back, but the ambulance driver put out his hand to stop him. 'Sorry, *señor*, but nobody's allowed inside with her.'

'But I'm her husband.'

'I'm sorry, *señor*. I'm taking her to the Hospital Clinico, in Málaga. You can visit her there.'

Velázquez considered chinning the guy. But if he did that, then the guy wouldn't be there to make sure Ana received any treatment she might need during the drive to the hospital, would she?

Finding himself in two minds, caught between wanting to punch the man, and figuring it might be wiser not to, Velázquez did nothing as the man closed the doors. And the next moment, the ambulance drove away.

Velázquez ran out and climbed into his car, but by the time he'd started it up the ambulance was nowhere to be seen. The ambulance man had said they were taking her to the Hospital Clinico in Malaga. Velázquez didn't know the hospital. He didn't know the city very well, either, even though he had been there a few times. But he knew it wasn't all that far away. Just a ten or fifteen-minute drive along the coast, he thought, as he headed out of the car park. And the hospital shouldn't be hard to find. Just a matter of keeping an eye out for the road signs, he told himself, as he headed up to the next roundabout, then joined the motorway and really put his put down.

He wondered why the driver hadn't taken Ana to a hospital in Torremolinos. Maybe they didn't have one. Torremolinos was just a small coastal resort, after all, while Málaga was a proper city.

Besides, even if there were a hospital in Torremolinos, the one in Málaga would be bigger and better equipped.

He hadn't driven far before he saw a sign for the Hospital Clinico and turned off. He found himself heading through the middle-class barrio of Teatinos, with its broad streets and modern apartment blocks. Then he saw the hospital, a big white building.

He drove into the car park, parked any old how, jumped out and ran over to the exit and in through the automatic doors. 'I need Emergencies,' he told the man behind the reception counter. The man asked for his name and *carné*.

Velázquez flashed his ID. 'Just tell me where Emergencies is.'

'Out through that door, then turn left and it's the second on the right.'

Velázquez dashed off, following the directions he had been given, and entered Emergencies. 'I'm looking for Ana Velázquez Becerra,' he told the man behind the reception desk. 'She was brought here in an ambulance.'

'We've got somebody's just been brought in after a car crash.'

'Ana Velázquez Becerra's a bullfighter. She took a goring at a *corrida* down in Torremolinos.'

The man shook his head. 'We haven't had any bullfighters in here this evening.'

Velázquez found a doctor and asked him if he'd seen Ana. No.

He asked several of the nurses on duty. No.

His heart was going crazy in his chest. Figuring the ambulance driver could have changed his mind about where to take her, Velázquez tried calling the other hospitals in Málaga.

Ana wasn't in any of them.

He called all the hospitals in the region, stretching all the way from Nerja to Marbella.

Nothing.

Velázquez wondered if he'd been tricked. He told himself not to jump to conclusions.

The trouble with this job, you got into the habit of expecting the worst.

He returned to the reception desk and showed the man sitting behind it his ID. 'I need you to contact all the ambulance drivers in the area, and find out if one of them is carrying Ana Velázquez Becerra, the bullfighter. She was badly gored at the *corrida* in Torremolinos earlier this evening. They put her in the back of an ambulance, and the driver told me he was bringing her here.'

'So maybe the ambulance is on its way.'

'It left the bullring before I did. And I've been here over fifteen minutes now,' Velázquez said. 'It doesn't take that long to get here. It's only a short drive.'

The man told him to wait a moment, then went off somewhere. When he returned, shortly afterwards, he looked at Velázquez and shook his head. 'There isn't any ambulance out there in the area carrying an Ana Velázquez Becerra.' The man shrugged. 'There's a record of an ambulance having been called out to the *plaza de toros* in Torremolinos, to collect a lady bullfighter who'd been gored. But there was no bullfighter there when the ambulance arrived.'

'What do you mean?'

'According to what I've just been told, she'd already left.'

Velázquez's heart sank.

Someone had taken Ana.

The question was, who?

Velázquez went back out into the car park and climbed into the Alfa Romeo. As he turned the key in the ignition, a huge tsunami of solid emotion racked his entire being. He began to sob.

When he'd cried himself out, he dried his eyes with the backs of his hands and set off. Minutes later, he was on the motorway heading for Seville. He drove with his foot on the floor all the way.

As soon as he got home, he found the bottle of Scotch and poured himself a large one. He knocked it down fast and poured himself another.

His mobile began to vibrate and slither over the sofa, like a sidewinder over the desert sand. He snatched it up. '*Hola*?'

A voice Velázquez didn't recognize said, 'We have your wife, Inspector Jefe.'

'Who are you?'

'That is not the question you should be asking yourself.'

'Is she all right?'

'Yes, she is perfectly safe.'

'Who are you? Why have you taken her?'

'All in good time.' The man's accent had a Russian twang to it.

'Listen, you crazy son of the great whore, she was badly gored. She's going to die if she doesn't get expert medical attention.'

'There's no need to worry on that score, I can assure you. And for your information, I am not a crazy maniac but a businessman. Do as I say and you will get your precious wife back unharmed. It's your choice.'

'But she needs to be in a hospital. The wound could infect.'

'I told you, there's no need to worry. Our surgeon has patched her up like new. Your wife is just fine.'

Velázquez swallowed.

'We'll be in touch. And listen, Inspector Jefe, you need to play this one alone if you ever want to see your wife alive again, you understand? No cops, okay?' the man said. 'Except you, of course.'

'Okay, no cops. But why did you take her? Is this your pathetic and stupid way of trying to get at me?'

The caller had already hung up

Now what?

We'll be in touch. They must want something from him. And presumably it wouldn't be long before Velázquez found out what it was.

He was angrier than he'd ever been in his life. He looked at his mobile like it was a poisonous snake and shat in the milk.

Then it began to ring again. '*Diga?*'

But this time it was only Gajardo. Velázquez's heart sank.

'Nothing much to report, boss,' the Subinspector said. 'None of the Russian students recognized the face in the portrait. But I just thought I'd call to ask how Ana got on in the *corrida*?'

'I'm living out a nightmare, José,' Velázquez told him, and explained.

They both went quiet for a moment and then Gajardo said, 'So what do we do now?'

'There's nothing to do except wait for the guy to call again.'

'Did he say when to expect his call?'

'No, just that he'd be in touch. And he said they had a doctor of their own looking after Ana, and that she's going to be fine.'

Silence.

Velázquez took a swig of his Scotch.

'What d'you reckon they want, boss?'

'That's what I've been asking myself, José.'

'What makes you so sure it's the Russians?'

'The man's accent, for one thing,' Velázquez said. 'Besides, who else can it be?'

'Could be Diego Blanco. He could've got a guy with a Russian accent to make the call, just to put you off the scent.'

'It's a possibility, I suppose.'

'Are you at home now, boss?'

'*Sí.*'

'Want me to come over?'

'There's no point.'

'Is there anything I can help you with?'

'No, I'll get back to you as soon as the kidnappers call again,' Velázquez said. 'Listen, José, not a word about this to anyone, okay? I'm gonna handle it my way.'

'Are you sure that's the best way to go about it?'

'I'm sure,' Velázquez said. 'You may as well grab some sleep. We're both gonna need to be fresh and wide awake first thing tomorrow.'

They said *buenas noches* and hung up.

Velázquez's head began to spin. He took deep breaths, and willed himself to calm down and get a grip.

He had to remind himself that he was an experienced police detective: Inspector Jefe del Grupo de Homicidios, no less. But somehow all his experience seemed to count for nothing right now.

He'd never had to work on a case in which someone he loved was taken from him. Velázquez realized that his own emotions were his worst enemy right now. The very love that he felt for Ana was working against him. He needed to approach this case with the same cool professionalism that he was known for, and he needed to eliminate the personal element.

He mopped the sweat from his forehead; then, feeling again as if somebody had put their fist into his belly and proceeded to squeeze and twist his guts, he dashed to the toilet and retched into the bowl.

Once he'd emptied the contents of his stomach, he splashed cold water over his face and hair and looked at his reflection in the mirror. He told himself he was going to get Ana back safe and sound if it was the last thing he did.

What now? he wondered. Then realized, once again, that there was nothing he could do.

He hated having to be passive. He wanted to be able to get out there and do something. Anything that would get him closer to finding Ana.

But all he could do was wait.

They'll call me, he told himself. They have to. They wouldn't kill her.

Why should they murder a woman just because she was living with him, after all?

No, this was just meant to be a warning. But it didn't make sense.

He told himself to stop thinking this way and start thinking like a cop. They must want something. Yes, that much was clear.

But what was it they wanted?

His mobile began to ring again. Maybe it was the kidnapper. He snatched it up. '*Diga*?'

'Luis, it's me,' said the familiar voice of his friend, Juan Gómez. 'I heard on the News that Ana's been gored. I'm so sorry. Where did the horn go in?'

'Just below the ribs, I think.'

'Was she conscious when they took her in the ambulance?'

'No.'

Silence.

'Below the ribs is the worst place to get it, right?'

Gómez said, 'Now listen to me, it was Ana's choice to become a bullfighter and you've been against it all along, so stop beating yourself up about it, Luis. It's not your fault this has happened.'

'No, but I'm scared she won't pull through.'

'Of course she will.'

They both went quiet.

'You're going to have to learn to calm down a little, *hombre*,' Gómez said. 'This sort of thing's going to happen from time to time, you know. It's practically an occupational hazard where bullfighters are concerned. You're just going to have to live with it.'

'I guess you're right.' Velázquez wondered whether to tell him that Ana had been kidnapped, but then figured there was no point.

'You need to try to stay calm, *amigo*,' Gómez said. 'Do some of those deep breathing exercises I showed you. That's the best thing to help you relax. Remember how to do them?'

'Sure. I'll try it now.'

'Is there anything I can do for either of you?'

'I'll tell you if there is.'

'You do that,' Gómez said. 'And try to take your mind off it – do something else…read, catch up on old stuff. Do anything so as long as you stay busy and stop brooding. And do remember to keep me posted, won't you?'

'Of course.'

They hung up, and Velázquez began to do the breathing exercises Gómez had talked about. He spent some twenty minutes on them. When he'd finished he remembered Lucia Segura's manuscript sitting there on the bookshelf. He went over and picked it up.

… The man I helped back to the safety of his family and comrades told everyone I had been fighting for the Republican army at Gandesa, and that I had saved his life when he was wounded. I explained that I had lost my papers in the fighting, which was easily accepted. Reinforcements had been sent to join the Nationalists, so the result of the battle was a foregone conclusion. Rather miraculously, then – or so it seemed to me – my conversion to the Republican cause was complete and quite free of complications. Just so long as I didn't come face to face with any Nationalists who knew me from my former life, I had nothing to fear…

Velazquez read on, about Pedro's life with his fellow Republicans – or maquis, as they came to be called – in the mountains. He read about how Pedro escaped into France in 1950 and didn't return to Spain until 1979, by which time it had become a democratic country – in name, at least…

Maybe he should never have come back, Velázquez found himself thinking. Because it seemed like someone could have been waiting to catch up with him.

The Inspector Jefe's mobile began to vibrate.

Chapter 15

'Velázquez,' came the familiar voice of Comisario Alonso, with its nasal Sevillano accent. 'We got another couple of bodies, in Calle Vidrio.'

One thought flashed through Velázquez's mind: Please, God, don't let it be Ana...

He said, 'Are the victims male or female?'

'Both male.'

Relief flooded through him.

Gajardo's old BMW was already at the crime scene, along with a patrol car, when Velazquez arrived.

The flat was on the top floor. There was no lift, and it was quite a way up. He had a fair amount of Scotch inside him, coupled with more grief and anxiety than he'd ever known, and was a little out of breath by the time he reached the top.

The door to the flat was ajar. Velázquez took a moment to get his breathing under control, before he went in, calling out '*Hola?*' as he did so.

'In here, boss,' Gajardo's familiar voice called back. Velázquez walked to the end of the hallway and entered one of the bedrooms. Two bodies were lying on the bed. Both naked. Both male.

Both very dead.

There was blood all over the place: over the sheets, the carpet, the walls. The victims were both in their twenties. One got it in the side of the head, the other in the chest. The arm of one was draped over the chest of the other.

The one shot in the head was Ramón Ochoa. Velázquez didn't even know the man had been released from the Hospital de la Macarena. And hadn't Ochoa been under arrest while he was in there, and chained to the bed? None of it seemed to make any sense.

'They caught up with him in the end,' Velázquez said with a grimace, as he turned to Gajardo.

The Subinspector nodded. 'I've searched the flat, boss,' he said. 'There's no sign of the murder weapon.'

'Did you check the trouser pockets of the victims?'

'Not yet, boss.'

Velázquez heard heavy footsteps and then he turned to see the Judge, Cristobal Montero, come into the room. Montero acknowledged the Inspector Jefe with a nod of the head and said, *'Buenos días,'* and the two officers responded in kind.

Velazquez wanted to ask Gajardo what he knew, if anything, about how Ramón Ochoa could have ended up here. But he was loath to parade his ignorance in front of Judge Montero.

Cristobal Montero ran a chubby hand through his salt-and-pepper hair and let out a sigh. His intelligent brown eyes fixed Velázquez with a thoughtful look.

Velázquez felt his head spin, and figured he probably smelt like the back end of a bender. A mint would come in handy.

Seeing Velázquez searching his pockets, the Judge reached into his jacket and brought out a packet of Marlboros, then offered Velázquez the pack. He declined. 'No, thanks, I quit years ago.' Cristobal Montero lit one up and took a drag.

Velázquez was surprised to see the man smoking here, at the scene of a crime. Not that he was about to say anything: rank was rank, after all. But he was irritated by Montero's casual arrogance and lack of professionalism.

He heard footsteps outside in the hallway and turned in time to see Gómez enter the room. The Médico Forense gave Velázquez a friendly slap on the shoulder. 'This city's getting to be like Chicago, huh?' he said and set about his work.

Two members of the Científico team came in. One of them got down on his knees and started drawing yellow circles round the spots of blood on the carpet, while the other concerned himself with the blood on the bedsheets.

The presence of the Científicos at the crime scene meant that Velázquez would have to limit himself to playing the role of spectator, something he hated.

If only he'd got here a little earlier, he could have searched the victims' pockets. But now it was too late. He would have to leave that to someone else, and wait to hear what was discovered, if anything.

The Judge's brow constricted, so that a triangle appeared above the bridge of his nose. 'Can you tell me anything about these two victims, Inspector Jefe?'

'The name of the lad who was shot in the back of the head's Ramón Ochoa, Judge. He was being framed for murdering the two priests. Then whoever tried to frame him stole my car and used it to drive at him, in an attempt to frame me for his murder. He was in a coma for a while, but he survived.'

'Not for very long, though, Inspector Jefe.'

'Unfortunately his luck ran out.'

'Okay, so assuming what you've just told me is correct, who was doing the framing. Any ideas?'

'It has all the signs of a turf war.'

'So you think all of the murders are linked, including that of the Russian?'

'I'd put this month's salary on it, if I were a betting man.'

'We're not running a betting shop here, Inspector Jefe, and nor is the court. I can't build a case by basing my investigation on luck.'

'I'm well aware of that, Judge.' Velázquez had to work to conceal his irritation. 'We've been working round the clock and doing everything we can, and we'll continue to do so. But we just need more time.'

Gajardo said, 'But these two latest victims were gay, boss.'

'So?'

'They hardly look like your typical pair of gangsters to me.'

Velázquez glared at his number two and said, 'When are you going to stop thinking in stereotypes, José?'

The Inspector Jefe went over to Gómez and said, sotto voce, 'What can you tell me about the time of death, Juan?'

'The temperature of the bodies suggests they were both killed sometime between eight and twelve hours ago. What's more, anal sex took place.'

'A regular Romeo and Juliet,' said Gajardo, who had come over to listen in.

'I heard that, Subinspector,' Judge Montero said, 'You're lucky it's me here and not Ernesto Sanz Rivera.'

Gajardo gave him a questioning look.

'Slightest hint of homophobia and he'd have your balls in a sling.'

'Gay, is he, Judge?'

'No, but he hates bigots. He sees them as a hangover from the bad old days of the Franco era...that whole homophobic Lord Of the Flies mentality.'

'*Que?*'

'It's the title of a novel.' Velázquez batted away a mosquito with his hand. 'A group of bigger schoolboys hunting the smaller ones on a deserted island.' He knew this because Ana had read the book and told him about it. Velázquez might not be much of a reader, but he was a good husband. And as such, he listened to what his wife had to say when she talked. And given that Ana was a bibliophile, Velázquez had enough information on important books stored away in his memory to sound relatively well read when it suited him to do so.

'And do they catch them or what, boss?' Gajardo asked.

'Yes, and they end up cooking one of them on a spit.'

Gajardo manfully volunteered to handle the prickly job of informing Señora Ochoa of her son Ramón's death. Velázquez could hardly go himself, given the highly sensitive nature of his involvement. He was left instead with the job of speaking to the neighbours in the block.

He rang the bell to the flat next door, and had to wait a while before an old man in a plaid dressing gown and slippers came and opened up. Velázquez showed the man his ID, and apologized for waking him. 'There's been a double murder next door,' he said.

The old man's mouth opened, revealing a couple of lonely yellow molars while his thick grey brows pointed to twenty to four.

'I just wondered if you heard anything, *señor?*'

'No…but when did it happen?'

'We can't be totally certain. But we think sometime between around three and seven p.m. Were you home at that time?'

The man nodded.

'But you didn't hear or see anything?'

'No, nothing at all.'

'What kind of person was your neighbour?'

'I saw him come and go.' The man shrugged. 'We'd say *buenos días* and that was it.'

Velázquez thanked the man and apologized again for waking him.

'I only wish I could help,' the man said.

Velázquez spoke to all of the neighbours on the top floor, then to the people who lived on the floors below. Nobody had heard or seen a thing. The killer probably used a silencer, Velázquez thought, as he made his way back out to his car.

The street was quiet as a stage set with no actors on it. Yet up there on the top floor of the building he'd just left, two young men had been murdered.

And Ana had been taken.

Juan Gómez had said the city was becoming like Chicago. Something strange was going on for sure. Seville was normally one of the most peaceful of places.

Velázquez started the engine up, buzzed the windows down and set off for home. But before he got there, he decided he couldn't face the place without Ana. So he just drove around the streets.

He figured he must have drunk the best part of a bottle of Scotch earlier, and yet he felt more or less sober now. All the shock and stress, he supposed. It had the effect of neutralizing the alcohol in your system.

His mobile began to vibrate in his pocket.

Chapter 16

'It's me, Luis.'

'*Hola*, Juan. What's new?'

'We've got an ID for the other victim. His name's Arturo Villanueva. His *carné* was in his trouser pocket.'

'I'll need his ID number, too.'

'Sure. Have you got pen and paper to hand?'

'Fire away.' Velázquez made a note of the number, and thanked Gómez. Juan was a true friend, as well as a great colleague, and as such he often passed on to Velázquez any information he happened to come by that might strictly be outside his job description as Médico Forense.

They hung up, and Velázquez continued to drive around the city's semi-deserted streets. Then his mobile began to ring again. He grabbed it, thinking it could be the kidnapper this time. But instead he heard Gajardo's familiar voice and heavy Sevillano accent coming down the line. 'Has the guy called back?'

'No, not yet, José,' Velázquez said. 'I'll let you know when he does.'

'I wanted to ask you earlier, but couldn't with the Judge and everyone there.'

'Did you tell Pilar Ochoa about Ramón?'

'*Sí.*'

'Thanks for doing that, José. How did she take it?'

'She said she was going to make sure you go to prison for his murder. I tried to tell her your car was stolen, and that whoever drove it at her son stole it with that purpose in mind – to frame you.'

'What did she have to say to that?'

'She told me I was lying, and just kept saying she knew I was covering for you because you're my boss. It's what cops always do, she said.'

'That's not a million miles from the truth in a number of cases I can think of.'

'I was with the woman for some time, but she was too upset to see reason. You do know she complained to Comisario Alonso, saying it was your car that drove at Ramón? That's why the Comisario gave the order to take the cuffs off.'

'I wasn't even aware he'd been released from hospital.'

'He discharged himself – very much against the doctor's orders. The lad clearly had the constitution of a *toro*.'

'And about as much brains. He should've listened to the doctor.'

'Might still've been alive if he had.'

'He might,' Velázquez said. 'Then again, whoever it was that killed him was determined to get to him, one way or another. It was only a matter of time.'

'I guess you're right.'

'Juan Gómez just called.'

'What was that about?'

'Does the name Arturo Villanueva mean anything to you?'

'No. Should it?'

'He's the other victim that was lying on the bed with Ochoa.'

'Oh…no, it doesn't ring any bells.'

'Nor with me,' Velázquez said. 'Listen. I want you to have Serrano or Merino positioned in an unmarked car outside the door to the block where Pilar Ochoa lives, as soon as they show up.' He glanced at his watch. It was coming up to 5.30. 'I want photographs of everyone who enters and leaves the property. And if you can put names to the faces, so much the better.'

'Are you sure that's doable, boss? A fair number of people must live in that block.'

'I guess you're right.' Velázquez just didn't have the manpower at his disposal to check out every person who happened to go in and out of a big block of flats like that. 'Anyway, we just need to do the best we can.'

The baroque façade of the Maestranza flashed by as he headed up the Paseo Cristobal Colon. 'Where are you now, José?'

'At home,' Gajardo said. 'I couldn't sleep. Been worrying about Ana too much.' He paused a beat. 'Are you sure it wouldn't be better to get the sound men over to listen in on the conversation when the kidnapper gets back in touch, boss? You never know, they might be able to trace the call.'

'No, I wanna do this my way. Remember what I said – no one's to know about it, okay? You're the only person I've told.' Actually, you're the second person, Velázquez thought. Diego Blanco was the other one. Velázquez had practically bitten his head off at the time. But the man didn't seem like he knew anything about it.

'Okay, boss. I'll call you later.'

'And let me know if anything happens, José.'

'You too, boss.' They hung up.

Velázquez started to feel sick. He returned to his flat to take his shot of methadone. Then he began to pace up and down the living room. His head was full of thoughts of Ana.

And for some reason, he found himself thinking of his first wife, Pe, and how happy he'd been with her all those years ago, before she was killed in the bullring.

After a while the sun came up. Then his mobile began to ring again. Velázquez picked it up. '*Diga?*'

'I want the CD-Rom, Inspector Jefe.'

'You're saying it's a film you want?'

'That's right. Vladimir Vorosky's CD-Rom.'

'But I don't have any CD-Rom,' Velázquez said.

'I am more than a little surprised by your attitude, Inspector Jefe. I had been under the impression you were in love with your wife, and that you valued her life.'

'I'll do anything you want...but what's this about a CD-Rom?'

No response.

Velázquez said, 'Look, if I had this CD-Rom of yours then I'd gladly give it to you in exchange for Ana. But I don't know anything about it.'

'Then that's just too bad, Inspector Jefe.'

'What do you mean by that?'

'I'm going to call you at the same time tomorrow on this number. If you have not acquired the CD-Rom by then you will never see your wife again.'

'Listen to me.'

But the man had already hung up.

Velázquez felt as though a fist had thrust itself into his belly and twisted his guts. He dashed to the bathroom and vomited into the sink. He retched again and again, until there was nothing left in his stomach. Finally he straightened up, and looked into the mirror, gripping the sides of the sink with his hands. His face was pale, unhealthy-looking, and he was weak in the knees.

He splashed some water onto his face, then went into the kitchen. He made himself a strong mug of coffee and paced the flat, sipping his coffee as he did so, and trying to work out how he was going to find the CD-Rom.

Vladimir Vorosky's CD-Rom, the man had said.

Was that why Vorosky had been killed? For a CD-Rom? But what could be on it that was so important?

Velázquez felt the sick feeling rising up in him again, and told himself to get a grip. He was not going to be any use to Ana unless he could keep his emotions under control. But that was easier said than done.

What I could do with now, he thought, is some heroin: the proper stuff.

That would help him keep his emotions in check.

He pushed the thought out of his mind: don't give in. Don't let them win.

The kidnapper had called on the stroke of nine. He'd said he would call again, the same time tomorrow.

I've got twenty-four hours to get this fucking CD-Rom, Velázquez thought, or Ana's going to die.

He knew he had to do what the man wanted – and fast.

But a large part of him was panicking. He had to find a needle in a haystack, only in this case the haystack was as big as Spain, bigger even perhaps. And he didn't have the first idea about where to start looking.

Through all the fog and fear, a name suddenly crystallized in his mind: Ramón Ochoa. The man might be dead, but more and more he seemed central to the case.

It might be an idea to go and talk to Ochoa's mother again. If Ramón was at the heart of all the mayhem somehow, then Pilar might know something she hadn't told him, some vital piece of information that she herself might not even realize was important but which could, with any luck, help Velázquez find the CD-Rom.

He realized that he was clutching at straws, but right now there was nothing else around for him to clutch at.

No sooner had she opened up and seen who it was than Pilar Ochoa tried to slam the door in Velázquez's face. He was too quick for her, though, and managed to get his foot in the jamb. 'What you don't seem to realize,' he said, 'is that I was batting for Ramón all along.'

Pilar Ochoa's eyes were brimming with venom. 'Ramón was innocent. First you set him up and then you tried to kill him. When you found out he was in a coma, you went back and finished the job.'

'No, you're wrong. It wasn't me. Somebody stole my car and used it to run him over, as well as to frame me while they were at it. It was the same people who tried to frame Ramón for Father Pedro Mora's murder. Then when Ramón recovered, they went back and killed him. But it wasn't me, I swear. Ramón knew that. I explained it all to him when I went to see him in the hospital, and he saw the sense in what I was saying.'

Pilar Ochoa appeared to take a moment to think about this.

'All I want is to talk, Señora Ochoa. I'm a police detective, not a killer.'

Velázquez could see from the look in the woman's eyes that she wasn't sure whether or not to believe him.

'Okay,' he said, 'I'll tell you something that I haven't told anybody. The people who killed Ramón have kidnapped my wife. They say they want a certain CD-Rom that belonged to a Russian by the name of Vladimir Vorosky, and I'm to get it for them by nine o'clock tomorrow morning. If I fail to deliver, I'll

never see my wife again. Now I love my wife very much…
What I've just told you is all true. You've got to believe me.'
There was a pause. His heartbeat counted out the seconds as
Pilar wavered: one, two, three, four…

'Okay,' she said, 'you'd better come in.'

Velázquez entered the flat and was assailed by the smell of
mothballs and polish, as Pilar Ochoa led him along a narrow
parquet hallway into the small living room, off to the right.
There were a number of religious icons on the shelves, and
paintings of Biblical scenes crowded the whitewashed walls.
'Take a seat,' she said, and pointed to one of the two easy chairs.
Velázquez told her he'd just as soon stand.

He was in a race against the clock, and felt better when he
was on his feet.

The noises of the street washed in through the open window:
a car going by, a man calling to a friend, a woman laughing.

'So what is it you want from me?' Pilar Ochoa brushed a few
stray hairs out of her eyes.

'I'm trying to find the person or persons who killed Ramón
and his friend. But to do that I'll need to ask you some questions
first, and I'm going to need some honest answers.'

'Okay, fire away.'

'I need to know if Ramón knew Father Pedro Mora, the priest
that was killed.'

'No, he didn't know him, but he was quite friendly with the
other one there,' she said. 'The young one with brown hair that
wears glasses.'

'Father Antonio, do you mean?'

'That's the one. Ramón was an addict, and the priest was
trying to help him kick the habit. He got him taking methadone
instead.'

'So Father Antoni was a good influence on your son?'

'So far as I could make out, yes.'

'And they were quite friendly, you say?'

'They seemed to be.'

'Can you tell me anything about the other two priests who
were killed?'

'No, I never heard Ramón talk about them.'

Velázquez thanked Pilar Ochoa for her help and went out. His mobile began to ring just as he was climbing into his car: it was Gajardo.

'Any news, boss?'

'The kidnapper called on the stroke of nine.'

'What did he have to say?'

'He wants Vladimir Vorosky's CD-Rom.'

'Come again?'

'That was my initial reaction,' Velázquez said. 'Anyway, we've got twenty-four hours to find it. If I don't have it by nine a.m. tomorrow then I'll never see Ana again.'

'Where are you now, boss?'

'I'm about to go over to Jesús del Gran Poder, to talk to Father Antonio again.'

'You know what they say about great minds,' Gajardo said.

'You mean you were already heading there, too?'

'I just parked outside and thought I'd call you.'

'Wait for me there,' Velázquez said. 'We'll talk to him together.'

Chapter 17

They found Father Antonio arranging some flowers up on the altar. '*Hola*, Father,' Velázquez said. 'We need to talk some more.'

The priest's thick brows rose in bushy curlicue. 'How can I help you?'

'I know that you're a big fan of marriage, Father.'

'I am indeed...but what's all this about?'

Velázquez said, 'My wife's been kidnapped. The kidnapper says he will call me again at nine tomorrow morning. I need to have acquired a certain object by that time. Otherwise he assures me I'll never see my wife again.'

'Oh no...but this is awful.'

'I haven't got much time.'

'No, of course not...but I really don't see how I can help.' Then he gave the Inspector Jefe a sly look. 'Unless you mean that you'd like me to pray for her?'

Velázquez said, 'You knew Ramón Ochoa rather well, Father, didn't you?'

Father Antonio's eyes flashed with alarm. 'What's all this about?'

'Why didn't you tell us that you knew him?'

'I'm sorry, but I don't follow.'

'Come on, Father, stop trying to pretend you don't know anything,' Velázquez said. 'Ramón's been murdered and I've just come from his mother's place. She told me that you'd befriended him. You were trying to help him kick his heroin habit.'

'That's right. But what's that got to do with anything?'

Velázquez wasn't sure yet, but he sensed there must be some kind of connection. 'Perhaps we should go somewhere we can talk in private?'

'*Si,* of course. Come with me.'

Velázquez and Gajardo followed the priest off along the aisle, through to the sacristy, and on into the room they'd used during the Inspector Jefe's previous visit. Father Antonio sat on the other side of the large oak desk. 'Please sit yourselves down, gentlemen.'

The officers parked themselves on the two upright chairs. Father Antonio said, 'So you want to talk to me about Ramón Ochoa, is that it?'

Velázquez nodded. 'Ramón was involved in something big. He ended up paying for it with his life. And I think you know what it was, Father.'

The priest grimaced. 'I have to say I feel uncomfortable talking about this sort of thing,' he said. 'I don't like divulging things that have been said to me in confidence – even when the conversations took place outside of the confessional.'

'Father, the clock is ticking.'

'Okay. Ramón told me that he'd burgled a flat. He was very concerned…'

'Go on.'

'Look, I really don't know if I ought to be telling you this.'

'For God's sake, Father – '

Father Antonio clenched his fist. 'Okay, I'll tell you, but you're not to tell anyone else, understood?'

'Okay, but out with it.'

'Ramón told me he burgled a flat and found a dead man lying on the bed. The man had been shot in the head.'

'Was it the Russian, Vladimir Vorosky?'

'That's what he told me afterwards, yes.'

'And you're quite sure the name of the dead man was Vorosky?'

'*Si.*'

'Can I ask why you didn't report this to the police, Father?'

'I'm telling you now, aren't I?'

'At the time, I mean, as soon as Ramón told you what happened?'

'Your people had already discovered the body by then, so there didn't seem to be any point,' Father Antonio said. 'Ramón would have been arrested for burglary and possibly for a

123

homicide, too – one which he didn't commit. He confided in me, Inspector Jefe.' Father Antonio's chest heaved, and he puffed out his cheeks. 'Locking him up in prison was only going to harden a lad like that. I saw that much straightaway.'

'Since when has the clergy in this city seen fit to set itself up as judge and jury, Father?'

'It wasn't a question of that, Inspector Jefe. Ramón was basically a decent lad. I sensed he was at that stage still where he could go either way, you know?'

'That you might be able to save him from a life of crime, you mean?'

'Exactly.'

Velázquez mopped his brow with the back of his hand. 'Okay, so what else did Ramón tell you?'

'He found a briefcase at the crime scene and brought it away with him.'

'What did he do with it?'

'I was just getting to that,' Father Antonio said. 'I suppose he must've taken whatever money was in there. But he gave me a CD-Rom and asked me to keep it for him.'

Velázquez nearly jumped out of the chair. 'Where is this CD-Rom now? I need to have it. Do you have it here or at home?'

'But what on earth can be on it that could possibly be of such earth-shattering importance, Inspector?'

'I really don't know at this stage. That's why I need to take a look at it.'

'But I gave it to the Russian.'

Velázquez felt his knees go weak, so that he had to lay a hand on the table to prevent himself from falling. '*Que*?'

'He came and asked for it.'

'And you just gave it to him?'

'What else was I supposed to do?' Father Antonio said. 'It wasn't mine, after all.'

'No, precisely. It was stolen property, Father,' Velázquez said. 'And as such you should have handed it over to the police straightway. And when I say police in this particular instance, I mean myself.'

'But this man came calling saying that it was his and he wanted it back.'

'Who was this man?'

'I already told you, he was Russian. He said he'd let Vorosky borrow it,' Father Antonio said. 'Did I do the wrong thing?'

'Dammit, Father…' Velázquez slammed the side of his fist down on the desk. 'I hope you realize I could arrest you for this?'

'On what charge?'

'Receiving stolen property. Conspiring to conceal a serious crime. Perhaps even conspiring to commit a serious crime.' He would have thrown in for being a prize bloody idiot, too, if there had been such a charge.

'But that's ridiculous.' Father Antonio's bushy brows worked through some tricky moves. 'I was merely returning what had been stolen to its rightful owner.'

Velázquez had to make a huge effort to get his emotions under control. 'Had you ever seen this Russian before?'

Father Antonio shook his head. 'I'm sorry, but there's no way I could have known this CD-Rom was so important to – '

'What did the man look like?'

'He was of average build, late twenties, had short brown hair and spoke pidgin Spanish. And I remember he was wearing jeans and a T-shirt.'

Velázquez reached into his jacket and brought out the photocopy of the portrait the artist had drawn. He unfolded it and held it up for Father Antonio to take a look at. 'Is this him?'

'Why, yes.'

'You're quite sure about that?'

'Totally.'

So at least Velázquez now knew whom Father Antonio had given it to. That was a start. 'So what's on this CD-Rom, Father?'

The priest shrugged. 'I've no idea.'

'You didn't take the opportunity to have a look at it?'

'No,' Father Antonio said. 'Why should I have?'

Velázquez was so exasperated he could have throttled the man. 'But what do you think was on it?'

'How would I know?'

'Ramón didn't give you any idea as to its contents?'

'No, I'm afraid he didn't, Inspector. But what exactly is all this about, may I ask? And why is this CD-Rom of such interest to you?' Then, before Velázquez had time to answer, the priest said, 'Unless…' His eyes flashed with the light of recognition. 'You don't mean to say it's what the kidnapper means to trade your wife's life for?'

Velázquez's mobile began to vibrate in his pocket.

'*Hola*, Inspector Jefe.'

'Who is this?'

'We haven't met before.' The man spoke with a strong foreign accent: possibly Russian.

Velázquez said, 'What do you want?'

'I think we both want something, Inspector Jefe.'

Velázquez's heart was pounding like a herd of elephants. 'Who are you?'

'That doesn't matter. I am nobody important.'

'I take it you were a friend of Vladimir Vorosky, am I right?'

'No, you are not correct, but that is not significant.'

'What do you want?'

'It is what we both want, Inspector Jefe.'

'Where are you?'

'I heard about your wife.'

'I want to speak with her now.'

'You are misunderstand, Inspector Jefe. I am not the man who has take her.'

'Who, then?'

'It is Mr. Big.'

'You're Russian, aren't you?'

'Yes, I am Russian, too. But it is another Russian, the one who he is running the *puticlub* in Camas.'

'How do you know this?'

'My girlfriend she work there.'

'At the *puticlub*?'

'Yes. I go in and talk to her and she tell me about it. She hear one of them when they speak about your wife on phone.'

'And you want to get your girlfriend out of there, is that it?'

'Correct…she don't want to work there, but they force her. The bad Russian he like her very much. She is very beautiful, you see, Inspector. We are going out together when we both are living in Moscow. We are very much in love. We make our plans to be married, you understand. But then he take her, and he bring her over here to Spain with him. He put her in *puticlub* to work for him, and he make her do things with the men who go there. He make her do the things with him, too. That man he is an animal.'

'So you want your girlfriend back?'

'That's right…the same as you, Inspector Jefe. So you see, we both want same thing.'

'Why doesn't your girlfriend leave the *puticlub*?'

'She cannot. He keep her there. She terrified of him and his people. They will to kill her if she try to escape.'

'I sympathize with you, but what do you want me to do?'

'That is very simple, Inspector Jefe. I want you to get my girlfriend from *puticlub* and bring her to me.'

'But that might not be very easy.'

'I do not say it will be.'

Velázquez said, 'Okay, so that's what you want me to do. But what can you do for me?'

'The answer to that question also is very simple, Inspector Jefe. You bring me my girlfriend, and I give you CD-Rom.'

'You mean that you have it?'

'But of course. It is for that I phone you.'

'Where are you now?'

'That is not important.'

'I'd like to talk with you face to face.'

'So you can to arrest me, no?'

'Okay, so bring me the CD-Rom. Once I have it, I'll go and get your girlfriend for you.'

'I am sure that would please you, Inspector Jefe. Unfortunately your idea it is not pleasing for me. You see, I am not fool. First you must get my girlfriend and bring me her. And then I will give you CD-Rom.'

'What's on the CD-Rom?'

'I am not aware of what it is containing.'

'You're lying.'

'No, I do not see it, Inspector.'

'But you must have some idea why it's so important to the man who has kidnapped my wife?'

'I do not see it, I am telling you. I am not work for this man. I am not take interest in his business. All I know is that he is very bad man. Very, very bad. And he has my girlfriend. And she hear them saying things…things she should not hear but she do hear them, you are understand me, Inspector? About CD-Rom and Vorosky and your wife. She is in the bed with the bad man, and he think she is asleeping and he make phone call. But she only pretend to sleep.'

'I see…well okay, I'll do what you ask. But how will I know which girl is the right one, when I go to the *puticlub*? And how will I manage to get her out, if people are watching her?'

'That is easy question, Inspector. My girlfriend her name it is Lena. She is tall brunette. She have small tattoo of cherub on right shoulder. Her last name it is Kovalyov. I spell that for you.' The man did so, and Velázquez wrote it down. 'But you must not asking to see Lena Kovalyo when you go to *puticlub*. This is very important. If you are do that, they will to know you go there from me. You must asking for Rosa when you go there. That is name she have when she work.'

'Okay, and the answer to my second question?'

'That is not so very simple, Inspector Jefe. If I know how to liberate my girlfriend from *puticlub* myself then I can to do it. But I am not policeman. It is you that is policeman, Inspector. This is the big difference. I think you are agreeing with me.'

'Even so…a policeman can't just walk into one of those places and march out with one of the girls.'

'You must to do it, Inspector Jefe, if you want CD-Rom. It is the price I ask. My girlfriend for CD-Rom. You can do it, I think.'

They both went quiet for a moment, then the man said, 'When you have CD-Rom you can give it to Russian mafia man. Then he liberate your wife and everyone happy.'

'Except the Russian.'

'He will be happy when you are give him CD-Rom.'

'Yes, but he won't be happy about losing your girlfriend, will he?'

'No, but I do not want for him to be happy about that thing, Inspector. He's very bad man. I already told you this, I think.'

'Yes, but what I mean is, he will go after you.'

'We will go away very far where he can not find us.' 'That sounds like a good idea.'

The man said, 'So you are exchange me my woman for your woman, Inspector. A life for a life. This is fair, I think.'

'Yes,' Velázquez said. 'That's fair. But I need to get the CD-Rom as soon as possible, otherwise the kidnapper's going to kill my wife.'

'I think you must be moving so quickly, then.'

Another idea occurred to Velázquez. 'Who is this Russian Mr. Big, anyway?'

'I see what you are think, but it will not work, Inspector Jefe.' 'What?'

'You can not get to him. The Russian he has always his guards – and they are special guards, very much trained and with guns. Nobody can get to him.'

'But who is he? What's his name?'

'We can to talk about this 'nother time, if you want, Inspector – after you are bring me my girlfriend.'

'Okay, so where do you want me to take your girlfriend, once I get her out of the *puticlub*?'

'I call you one hour from now and give directions.'

Just then, the church bells began to ring, and Velázquez could also hear them ringing out of his mobile. The caller hung up.

Velázquez dashed out of the room, and on through the sacristy and into the main part of the church. His eyes roved over the people who were praying. Then he saw a man go out through the main exit. Medium build, short brown hair, dressed in jeans and a T-shirt, just as Father Antonio had described.

Velázquez dashed after the man, and caught up with him outside. 'Show me your ID,' he said.

The man appeared stunned. 'I beg your pardon?'

Velázquez took out his own ID and held it up, quickly introducing himself as he did so. 'I need you to show me your *carné de identidad, señor.*'

'What's all this about?' The man spoke with an accent that was as Andaluz as flamenco.

'I'm looking for somebody who meets your description, *señor.* Now, your *carné, por favor.*'

The man took out his ID card and handed it over.

Velázquez looked at it. The name on the *carné* was Enrique Sainz Romero. The man was clearly Spanish. 'Is there some problem?' he asked.

Velázquez handed the man his card and said, 'No, *gracias.*' Then he spotted another man at the other end of the square. He was average build, short brown hair, wearing jeans and a T-shirt. And he was clearly in a hurry. 'Stop!' Velázquez shouted. '*Policía!*' The man turned to look back, then speeded up.

Subinspector Gajardo emerged from the church at that moment, and called over to Velázquez. The Inspector Jefe pointed and shouted, 'Stop him!' then set off at a sprint after the man. Gajardo followed.

The man hopped onto a motorbike, then revved the engine. He glanced over his shoulder, but he was too far away for Velázquez to get a good look at his face. Besides, the man was wearing shades. 'You there, stop!' Velázquez shouted. '*Policía!*'

The man set off on his motorbike with a roar of the engine. Within seconds, he had reached the end of the narrow street, and Velázquez could only watch and curse as the vehicle turned the corner.

Gajardo drew level, shading his eyes as he looked up the street. 'Manage to get a look at his face, boss?'

Velázquez shook his head and shat on the forebears of the man who had just got away.

'So now what do we do?'

'I'll just have to do as the guy said, I guess.'

'What's that?'

'He wants me to spring his girlfriend from the *puticlub* over in Camas in return for the CD-Rom.'

'I gathered that from listening to you on the phone, boss.'
'Question is, how the fuck am I gonna do it?'

3

TERCIO DE MUERTE

The bull eyed the matador *with the cold stare of a killer – a killer that senses he is being outmanoeuvred, despite his vastly superior size and strength. And so there was a sense of caution and humiliation mixed in with his rage. Blood was running from the area in its neck, where the pics were lodged, as well as from his mouth. The bull was tired. Tired with the fight he'd be given. Tired of charging the cape over and over, only to find empty air. The animal wanted to put an end to it. You could see it in his eyes. It would come any moment now: the moment of truth.*

The bull stamped once, twice, three times; then the matador *cried,* 'Toro! Toro!'

Chapter 18

Half an hour later, Velázquez and Gajardo were sitting in Gajardo's car across the street from the Russians' *puticlub* out in Camas.

Velázquez turned to his number two. 'You stay here, José,' he said. 'And keep the engine running in case we have to make a fast getaway.'

'Sure you don't want me to go in there with you, boss?'

Velázquez shook his head. 'If I'm not back out within twenty minutes then you'd better call the cavalry.' He got out, crossed the street, and went in through the front entrance of the club past the blond gorilla on the door.

After the bright sun and intense heat of the street, the relative darkness of the small lobby was a shock to the senses. Velázquez passed through the padded swing doors, into a large bar. There were a couple of girls dancing on poles on a stage in the middle of the place, and there were booths around the walls, most of which were empty. It was a little early in the day to be doing much business, the Inspector Jefe presumed.

The clientele was made up of seedy-looking guys in their forties or fifties. As for the girls, they were young and mostly blondes from Eastern Europe. Velázquez got the attention of the bull working the bar. The guy must have weighed in at a good 130 kilos, all of it solid muscle, and had a short brush of blond hair that you could have used to sweep the floor, if he hadn't been the sort to break your neck if you tried it. Velázquez ordered a beer.

As the man bent down for a bottle, a girl appeared at Velázquez's side. She had the same short skirt, blonde hair and fake boobs as the rest of the girls in the place. Velázquez could tell her boobs were false because they were further apart than natural ones.

Arnie Schwarzenegger's twin set the cerveza down on the counter before Velázquez, along with a glass. Velázquez asked the man how much he owed for the beer. A thousand *pesetas,* the man told him. Which was about eight times what you'd pay in a normal bar. You could eat a three-course meal for that money in a lot of places. Still, it was all coming out of the Inspector Jefe's expense account.

He paid the man, conscious as he did so that the girl at his side had just put her hand on his thigh. 'You seem like my kind of man,' she said and smiled.

Looking at the girl's perfect teeth, Velázquez wondered how much the orthodontic work she'd had done must be costing her. She would be repaying the bills for the liposuction and her boob job, too. Then there was the cost of bringing her to Spain, and whatever her keepers spent on clothing and feeding her. And she'd be paying it all with interest. The way these guys generally operated, the debts the girls had to repay would turn out to be perpetual, eternal.

Velázquez looked into the girl's eyes, searching for signs of a real person in there, something that the girl's keepers hadn't beaten or terrified out of her. She should be suffering like hell. She should look scared or depressed, or even just sad. But she didn't. What she looked was horny.

He wondered if the girl was drugged up. He figured she had to be, poor kid. 'You wanna come upstairs with me, sailor?' she purred. 'I could float your dinghy,'

'I'm looking for Rosa.'

'What's the matter, don't you like me?' Her pout was a master class on false innocence. 'Ain't nothing Rosa can do for you that I can't do better, baby. Why don't you come upstairs and let me show you my map of India?'

'I want to see Rosa.'

The girl pointed along the bar to another blonde, who could have been her identical twin sister. The second girl looked over, saw the first girl gesturing and came to join them. 'Your friend's here,' the first girl said.

Velázquez smiled. 'You'd be Rosa, right?'

The second girl nodded. 'Hi, sugar. You been in here before?'

'No, but a friend of mine has and he recommended you. He said you knew how to show a guy a great time.'

'Your friend sounds like an intelligent man.'

'Oh, he's that all right.'

'What's his name?'

'Juan Rodriguez,' Velázquez improvised.

'I think I know the man you mean.'

The first girl said, 'Enjoy,' and made herself scarce.

'We will,' Rosa said. Then she looked at Velázquez: 'You wanna buy me a drink first, or'd you prefer to go to one of the rooms straightaway?'

'Going to one of the rooms sounds good.'

'Sure.' The girl set off and Velázquez followed her up the stairs. They went along a carpeted hallway, then the girl stopped outside one of the doors and knocked. Nobody answered, so they went inside.

'Wait a moment,' Velázquez said. 'Don't undress. I need to talk to you.'

The girl shrugged. 'Sure, whatever you fancy. So long as you realize it'll cost you the same.'

Velázquez looked at her. 'Your boyfriend sent me.'

A look of fear came into the girl's brown eyes.

'He wants me to take you to him now.'

'You're crazy as a goat.'

'He says he loves you and that you love him, is that right?' The girl was looking at Velázquez, but he could tell she didn't really see him. She was travelling back in time, through clouds of whatever drug it was her keepers filled her with. Her mind was taking her to the clean happy days when she and the man she'd been going to marry were seeing each other in Russia.

'He says nothing's changed,' Velázquez said. 'Everything's changed.'

'Not for him. He says he still loves you like the first day he saw you.'

The girl seemed to snap out of her reverie. 'Do you know what they will do if I try to get away from here and they catch us?'

'But he's going to take you somewhere far away... somewhere they'll never find you.'

Judging by the look on her face, conflicting emotions seemed to be fighting it out inside the girl. 'It's too dangerous.'

'Don't be stupid, Lena. This is your only chance of ever living a normal happy life.'

'Lena,' she said. 'He told you my name.'

Velázquez nodded.

'That's my old name. The one I used to have before I came here. Now I am Rosa.'

'It's not your old name, Lena. It's your real name. There is no Rosa. She's a made-up person. She was created by the monsters who brought you to Spain and keep you imprisoned here.'

The girl looked at him as if she were trying to summon the courage to hope.

'My friend is waiting for us in a car outside,' Velázquez said. 'Now what's the quickest way out of this place?'

'Out through the bar, the way you came in,' she said. 'But everyone will see us. They will stop us.'

'No, Lena.'

'Yes, they will. One of the other girls tried to leave and they stopped her. Then they beat her so badly afterwards she couldn't walk properly for a month.'

'That's not going to happen this time.'

'Have you seen Sergei, the gorilla they have for a barman?' she said. 'And then there is Boris, who is not so strong but he is so violent I think even Sergei is scared of him. There are many others like them, and they are all armed. You are no match for them, believe me.'

'Perhaps I should tell you that I'm a police detective.' Velázquez took out his ID and showed it to her. 'They'll have to let us leave.'

'Maybe, but I wouldn't bank on it. And even if we do get out of here, they'll track me and Fyodor down and kill us,' she said. 'I already told Fyodor this, when he came into the club to talk to me. I told him he should forget it and leave me.'

'They will never catch you. I promise you,' Velázquez said. 'You just need to be brave this one time, okay? Can you do that?'

The girl looked into Velázquez's eyes for what felt like ages, then she nodded.

'Are you ready to leave?'

'*Si*, all right.'

'Come on, then. Hold my hand and don't let go, whatever happens, all right?'

They left the room, then went back down the stairs. They had to cross the long bar, before they got to the padded swing doors. One of the bouncers came and blocked their path. The man had patchwork white and gold teeth, and eyes that looked like they'd been rented from the reptile house at the zoo. 'Where d'you think you're going?'

Velázquez said, 'I'm a police detective and I need to take this young lady in for questioning.'

'She don't know nothin'.'

'I'll be the judge of that.'

'What d'you want to question her about?'

'I have reason to believe that one of her clients is involved in a case of serious fraud.' Velázquez took out his ID and held it up. 'I'm afraid I can't tell you any more than that at this moment in time.'

The man snatched Velázquez's ID from his hand and took a close look at it. 'She's workin'.'

'Yes, I realize that. I won't keep her long.'

The man handed Velázquez's ID back to him, and looked as though he were in two minds about whether to allow them to leave. 'This is very irregular,' he said. 'Girls are not allowed to leave when they're workin'.'

'Can't be helped, I'm afraid...unless you'd like me to get the Vice Squad in here and shut the whole place down.'

'Hey, this place is legal.'

'Not sure my friends in the Vice Squad would agree, judging by some of your practices.'

'What practices?'

'It sounds from the way you're talking that you keep the girls who work for you here incarcerated.'

'They free to come'n go as they please.'

'Really?'

'Si…you only gotta ask any of them '

'In that case, you won't mind if I borrow Rosa for a few hours, then, will you?'

The man looked at the girl and said something in Russian, then he stood aside.

They hurried across the street and jumped into the back of Gajardo's car. 'Let's go,' Velázquez said. 'And step on it in case they change their minds and try to follow us.'

The Subinspector set off at speed, and glanced in his mirror a couple of times. 'Doesn't seem like anyone's coming after us, boss.'

Minutes later, when they were on the main road back to central Seville, Velázquez asked Lena what the gorilla had said to her in Russian before they left. 'He told me I'd be food for the fishes in the sea if I'm not back by seven o'clock this evening.'

It wasn't long before they reached the centre of the city. Gajarda had to slow down for a horse and carriage with a smartly dressed family in it to pass in front of them. Couples were sitting under the broad parasols at the tables spaced out along Calle Betis. 'Where are you taking me?' Lena asked.

'That's up to your boyfriend.'

Minutes later, Velázquez's mobile started to ring. '*Diga*?'

'It's me, Inspector Jefe. Have you got Lena?'

'*Si.*'

'Good *hombre*. Let me speak to her.'

Velázquez handed the phone to Lena, and listened to her talk in Russian. As she spoke, tears ran down her cheeks. She wiped them away with the back of her hand. Then she handed the phone back, and Velázquez asked the man where he wanted to meet up.

'I'm in house on road to Dos Hermanas,' the man said. 'I give you directions where to go, okay?'

The Russian had chosen to rent an isolated farmhouse where there would be no nosy neighbours around to see what he was doing. The place had been painted white, and the pitched roof was covered with red tiles. A small garden with a hedge surrounded the property, and then there was nothing but fields that led as far as the trees in the distance.

As they made their way over the gravel path, the front door opened. And on seeing her hero step out onto the doorstep, Lena rushed over to him. He swooped her up in his arms and they hugged in a passionate embrace. The man – Velázquez had heard Lena call him 'Fyodor' – began to say things to her in Russian.

Then Fyodor set her down on her feet. He turned to Velázquez and said, 'I am sorry, Inspector Jefe. You must please to excuse us. We are behaving like the children...but we are too happy.'

'I understand.'

Fyodor offered Velázquez his hand and they shook. 'I want to thank you for bring to me my Lena.'

Velázquez said, 'I just hope you're both very happy together.'

'Don't worry, we will be. But we must to go somewhere far away from here, where we can be safe.'

'That sounds like a sensible idea.'

'And who he is your friend?'

'Subinspector Gajardo, meet Fyodor.' The two men nodded at each other.

'Please.' Fyodor threw out his arm. 'Come inside.'

'I have no time to waste,' Velázquez said. 'I've fulfilled my side of the bargain. Now it's time for you to fulfil yours. I need the CD-Rom.'

'*Si,* of course...but please come inside and we can be doing our business there.'

Fyodor turned and led them in through the door, into a small hallway, and then off into the main living room. There was a brick fireplace with a natural coal fire, and framed drawings and paintings of country scenes adorned the whitewashed walls. 'Please sit,' Fyodor said.

'No, I've already told you I'm in a hurry. I want the CD-Rom.'

'And you will have it, Inspector Jefe.'

'I'm in no mood to be kept waiting around, Fyodor.'

'It is with my brother.'

'But that wasn't part of the deal.'

'I give to him for safe keeping.'

'Why on earth did you do that?'

'In case the people who was keeping Lena they catch me. I did not want to risk that they find CD-Rom.'

Velázquez's chest heaved as he worked to keep his temper under control. 'Listen to me, Fyodor. I went to the *puticlub* and got Lena out of there. I did so at some risk to both of us. There was no saying how the goons that run that place might behave. But I got her out and she's here. And you gave me your word you'd have the CD-Rom for me.'

'I do have it, Inspector Jefe…only not here. It is with my brother, Vassily.'

'So tell him to come here right now. My wife will be killed if I don't have the CD-Rom when the kidnapper calls at nine o'clock tomorrow morning. Do you understand that?'

'Yes, and you will have it. There is nothing for you to be worry about, you really must believe me.'

'So get your brother here.'

'Vassily is in Tarifa. We must go to him, and he will give you CD-Rom.'

Velázquez felt like he was about to lose his temper. But knocking this Fyodor character around would only slow him down. He took a deep breath and looked at his watch. He started to count. Got to five, and found that he had somehow managed to resist the urge to hit the man he was dealing with.

'There's plenty of time.' Fyodor smiled.

Velázquez said, 'So let's go.'

'Want me to come with you, boss?' Gajardo asked.

'No, you drive back to Seville, José. You're going to have to take charge while I'm gone. And keep me updated on what's happening, okay?'

'Will do, boss. Adios.' Gajardo went out.

Fyodor said, 'We can take my Volkswagen.'

Chapter 19

The euphoria that swept over Fyodor and Lena on finding themselves reunited had cooled into an edgy nervousness by the time they got on the road. Feeling irritated by the way the pair were chattering in Russian, Velázquez told them it would make him feel a whole lot better if they spoke in Spanish from now on. 'Makes me wonder,' he said, 'if you're both up to something that you don't want me to know about.'

Lena turned her head and smiled at the Inspector Jefe. 'I just said that the same car's been behind us for the past twenty minutes.'

'Nobody is on our tail, *guapa*,' Fyodor said. 'Is just going to same direction as we. Is only one road.'

Velázquez watched Fyodor as he peered in the mirror: the man's eyes were charged with about as much tension as jump leads.

Lena said, 'Why don't you let the man overtake?'

'Is no overtaking on this part of road.'

'Try it and see what he does.'

'Okay.'

So Fyodor slowed down, and it wasn't long before the driver in the car behind was flashing his lights at him. Then the man took a chance and overtook, driving at close to seventy kph into a bend. 'The Spanish drivers.' Fyodor laughed and shook his head. 'They sometimes is not have many patience, huh?'

Minutes later, they passed Gibraltar, the Rock rearing up out of the water like a huge craggy molar that almost seemed close enough to touch. It was hard to believe that people actually lived out their lives on that shapeless and inhospitable-looking piece of stone. Lena said she'd always wanted to go there. 'We go one time,' Fyodor said. 'But not today.'

'No, we won't. We'll never go there now, and you know it.'

'Hey, we free to go where we please, huh?'

'No, that's not true,' Lena said in a quiet voice.

'Hey, we just got you free from that place, and we together now. That is what is so important, huh?' Fyodor glanced at

Lena, as if to test the effect of his words on her. 'We go there to Gib one day, my darling, but not today, huh?'

'No, we'll never go there. Not now.'

Fyodor let out a sigh and shook his head.

They pressed on in silence, and it wasn't long before the road started to get bendier than a sleeping python. And somehow Velázquez had a strange, creepy feeling, like they were heading towards some lost stretch of land that the sea had spewed up long ago, but which civilization had yet to make its own.

'You are not saying so much, Inspector Jefe,' Fyodor said.

'Your brother had better be there with the CD-Rom. That's all that matters to me right now.'

'Of course. He wait there for us.'

Finally they reached the town of Tarifa and drove through its windswept streets. They passed the old castle walls, and when they came to the cathedral Fyodor pulled over. 'It's little pizza restaurant where Vassily he is waiting for us – near to cathedral, he say.'

They climbed out of the car, then walked round the back of the cathedral, and sure enough there was a pizza restaurant just up ahead. The warm wind that blew in off the sea was somehow full of echoes and secrets, and Velázquez's heart was playing hopscotch in his chest as they walked up to the corner.

There were a few people eating at plastic tables on the terrace. Velázquez told Fyodor to go in first. 'I'll be right behind you,' he said. 'And I've got my hand on my gun. It's in the pocket of my jacket, in case you're wondering. So take it real steady. No fast movements.'

'But there is no need for that, Inspector.'

'Let's hope not.'

They went inside like that, with Fyodor in front, Velázquez right behind him, and Lena making up the rear. The restaurant was a long, rectangular-shaped affair, and a large bear of a man, with short brown hair, was sitting alone at a table at the far end. His white face was broad and had a flattish, red, drinker's nose in the middle of it. The man got to his feet when he saw them, and looked very happy to see his brother. The two men hugged and kissed each other on the cheek.

'Look,' Velázquez said, 'this is all very nice, but I didn't come here to witness a family reunion. Where's the CD-Rom?'

'I have it here.' Vassily reached inside his brown leather jacket.

Velázquez did likewise and brought out his gun. He took a step forward and held it low against Vassily's belly.

'Fyodor told me you are a policeman,' Vassily said.

'That's right. Now sit at the table, nice and slowly, the three of you.'

They did as they were told, and Velázquez sat down with them, timing it so that he moved as they did. 'Right, now perhaps you ought to know that my gun is pointing at a part of your anatomy you probably value fairly highly, Vassily. You get my drift?'

Vassily nodded. 'But there is no need for this, Inspector.'

'It's just what you might call a precaution…in case either of you get the silly idea to try and trick me.'

'But I have the CD-Rom here.' Vassily held it up.

'You brought a laptop, like I said?'

'Yes – here.' Vassily pointed to a black case on the floor. 'I need to see it.'

'What…now?'

'That's right. Now. For all I know, the CD-Rom you've got there could be blank. Or else it could be a pirate copy of Mary Poppins.'

'Okay, no problem, Inspector Jefe. You can watch it now on my laptop.'

Fyodor said, 'Who she is, this Mary Poppins?'

Once he'd got back to Seville, Velázquez headed straight for Blondes. He parked, entered the club, and spotted Diego Blanco sitting on a stool at the bar. True to form, the man was holding court to a bevy of young women. It was all enough to make Velázquez want to puke. He shat in the milk under his breath as he made his way over to the counter, near to where the gangster was sitting. He got the attention of the barman and asked for a large Johnnie, neat. 'Black or red?' the barman asked.

'Black,' Diego Blanco called through the melee. 'And it's on the house.'

Velázquez turned and said, 'I see you've got company.'

The gangster shrugged. 'How's the business going with your wife?'

The barman put Velázquez's drink down on the counter. The Inspector Jefe picked it up and knocked it back in one. 'There somewhere we can talk in private?'

'Sure.' Diego Blanco picked up his gin and tonic and slid off his stool. The small sea of cleavages parted to allow him to pass. 'Come with me.'

Velázquez followed the gangster's squat form along the end of the bar. The man's ponytail was like a giant tadpole on the shoulders of a baby rhino, swishing back and forth as he walked. They passed through a door and into a small room. The gangster pushed a switch and the light came on. The walls were covered with red flock, and there was a mahogany desk and a couple of padded chairs.

'Take a seat.' Diego Blanco gestured with his hand, then parked his squat form in the black swivel chair.

Velázquez sat across the desk from the gangster, and took the CD-Rom from his breast pocket. 'You got a laptop handy?'

'What's this all about?'

'I need you to watch this with me.'

'What's on it?'

'It's the CD-Rom that Ramón Ochoa stole from the Russian, Vladimir Vorosky.'

'The Russian that was murdered, you mean?'

Velázquez nodded. 'Why did you order Ramón to steal it?'

'I didn't.'

'Come on, Diego, don't waste my time. If you want me to help you try and run the Russians out of town, then you're gonna have to scratch my back a little first.'

'I had Ramón watch Vladimir Vorosky.'

'Why?'

'Why do you think?' Diego Blanco said. 'I wanted to know what the man was up to.'

'Did you send Ramón to kill him?'

'No, not at all. Why should I have wanted Vorosky dead?'

'You tell me, Diego.'

'No reason at all. Fact is, Vorosky approached me. He said he wanted to split from his boss, Boris Kerensky.'

'Did he say why?'

'He just said Kerensky wanted too much for himself... man was a greedy fucker.'

'So Vorosky wanted what from you?'

'He wanted to come in with me.'

'Did you trust him?'

'You think I got to the top of the shit-heap by trusting people so easy as that?' Diego Blanco said. 'You wanna run a city like Seville, you need the balls of a *toro*, sure. But you also need the eyes of a fox. I wanted to find out what he was up to first, before I even considered his offer...which is why I had Ramón watch him.' The gangster took a sip of his drink.

'What decision did you come to in the end?'

'I didn't...he was killed before I had time to consider it properly.'

'You sent Ramón to burgle Vladimir Vorosky's place, didn't you?'

'Not exactly.'

'Good as told me so yourself, Diego.'

'I may have told Ramón the man was keeping some money there, but that's something different...'

'In a briefcase?'

'Possibly.'

'What about the CD-Rom?'

'What CD-Rom would this be?'

'This one here.' Velázquez held it up. 'Are you telling me you don't know anything about it?'

'You mind telling me what the fuck you're talking about?'

'Where's your computer?'

Diego Blanco opened one of the drawers in his desk and brought out a silver laptop. He placed it on the desk and booted it up. 'I still don't get what it is you want from me?'

'The truth, Diego.'

'I've just told you everything there is to tell. I don't know anything about any CD-Rom.'

The two men fell silent as they looked at each other across the desk. 'Vorosky was already dead when Ramón broke into the house. He took a briefcase and found a lot of cash in it and the CD-Rom. He gave the CD-Rom to a friend, and asked him to hold onto it for him.' Velázquez fed the CD-Rom in, then moved the laptop so they'd both be able to watch the footage. 'Perhaps I should warn you, Diego, it's not pleasant viewing.'

The Inspector Jefe glanced at the gangster from time to time, as they watched the footage, and he saw from the man's expression that the CD-Rom wasn't his idea of entertainment.

'This is fucking sick,' Diego Blanco said.

'But why'd the Russian want it so badly is what I don't get?'

'Either because he's on it, or to use it as blackmail material are the only explanations I can think of.'

'But how can it be for either of those reasons if you can't see the men's faces?'

'Don't you ever get to see them?'

Velázquez shook his head.

'In that case,' Diego Blanco said, 'I see what you mean. It's all a bit of a mystery.'

'I was hoping you might be able to help me.'

'How?'

'That you might know something I don't, I mean?'

'Sorry.' Diego Blanco sipped his gin and tonic. 'Solving mysteries isn't my line, Inspector.'

'It's creating them, you mean?'

'No need to get like that. I thought you'd come here to ask for my help?'

'Obviously that was a stupid idea.'

Velázquez took the CD-Rom out and put it back in his pocket.

'So when's the Russian gonna call you?'

'Nine o'clock in the morning.'

'You give him the CD-Rom and he hands your wife over, is that it?'

'That's the deal, yeah.'

'It's a very strange business, if you ask me. Sorry I can't help you. Truly I am.'

Velázquez was feeling clammy and like he was going to be sick. He realized that he needed a fix. Then he told himself he didn't need one, he just wanted one.

Okay, he wanted one badly, then…but he could beat this. He had the methadone to keep him going, and he was going to kick his habit. I am, he told himself.

I am.

He got up, trying his best to conceal his feelings of nausea.

Diego Blanco said, 'You don't look so good.'

Velázquez went out.

Chapter 20

Once he arrived at the Jefatura, Velázquez went in search of a tekkie. He got lucky and found Luz Cano. He gave her the CD-Rom and had her run the footage on a large screen.

'That poor kid can't be any older than thirteen,' Luz said. 'Maybe a year or two younger.'

'It's hard to tell without being able to see his face.' Velázquez blew out his cheeks. 'And we can't see the faces of any of the sick bastards that are doing it to him.' He held up his hand: 'Stop it there.'

Luz pushed the pause button, and Velázquez went up close to the screen. 'That piece of sculpture.' He pointed to a figurine that stood alone on the mantelpiece. 'Hone in on it for me.'

Luz magnified the figurine, so that it covered most of the screen. Velázquez scrutinized it. It was the only distinctive piece on view. All the other ornaments and pieces of furniture had been cleared away.

'What do you make of it, Luis?'

It was a black and white piece of a woman dancing. 'It's rather impressive.'

'Yeah,' Luz agreed. 'I like the way the sculptor worked the hair, like you can see the waves in it. And the way she's been caught in motion, too.'

'Looks real, doesn't it?'

Luz nodded, still looking at the image. 'I wonder if it's an original.'

'That's what I need to find out.'

'You think it might give you a clue as to where this took place, is that it?'

'If I can trace the seller and find out who he sold it to.'

'Sounds like a bit of a long shot.'

'Right now long shots are all I've got,' Velázquez said. 'That figurine's the only distinctive feature in the film, so far.'

'Don't forget the strawberry mark one of the guys has on his ass.'

'No, I noticed that, Luz. But it's gonna be kinda difficult to go around Seville asking men to drop their trousers so we can take a look at their asses.'

Luz nodded, and Velázquez told her he wanted to see the rest of the footage. And no sooner had it resumed than the Inspector Jefe felt the potent cocktail of anger and disgust return.

When the film ended, he had Luz run off a copy so he could take it with him. 'I've got to go and do something important now,' he said. 'But I'll need four more copies of the CD-Rom, and some blow-ups of the figurine and the people in the film, okay?'

'Sure,' Luz said. 'I just hope you catch those sickos.'

Velázquez took out his mobile and called his number two.

'*Hola*, boss. Jeez, what time is it?'

'Sorry about the hour, José. Did I wake you?'

'Yeah, but don't worry about it.'

One thing about Gajardo, you could call him any hour of the day or night and he was ready to spring into action.

'Did you get the CD-Rom okay, boss?'

'I've just watched it.'

'Learn anything?'

'Not much, apart from the fact that there's a group of perverts in Seville raping young boys.'

'Nothing to suggest who they could be?'

'One of them's got a strawberry mark on his ass, and that's it.'

'No faces?'

'No, they took care not to give themselves away like that,' Velázquez said. 'Although there is a small figurine in the background on the footage, which we might be able to trace if it's an original.'

'What do you need me to do?'

'Come and get the copies of the CD-Rom and the blow-ups from Luz Cano.'

'What about you?'

'I'm heading home to wait for the call from the kidnapper.'

'Okay, I'm leaving now,' Gajardo said. 'What I don't get, though, is why the kidnapper should want this CD-Rom if there are no faces on it?'

'That's what I've been trying to work out, José.'

'Are you still sure you don't want to get the sound guys over to your place, to see if they can trace the call when it comes?'

'No, I wanna do this my way, José.'

'Okay, boss. So call me as soon as you know anything, okay?

'Sure. Hasta luego.'

Velázquez told Luz that Subinspector Gajardo was on his way over, then he left the building and drove home. It was coming up to half-past five when he got back to the flat. He was shaking all over, and he only just reached the bathroom in time to puke into the tub, but too late to avoid soiling his pants.

Disgusted with himself, he undressed, cleaned up and dumped his dirty clothes into the washing machine. Then he fetched the baggie from its hiding place. He took out a fresh hypodermic needle, then went into the kitchen and heated the heroin. His heart pounded as he watched the heroin bubbling up in the spoon.

He was dying for it. Dying for this substance that would end up killing him if he let it. He was disgusted with himself. At the same time, a part of him was way past worrying about moral considerations or what he thought of himself. He was being pulled in opposing directions. His self-respect told him what he was doing was wrong. But his need for the heroin was greater than his self-respect.

He told himself this would be the last time. He would take it this once, to help him through. Just so he could do what had to be done to get Ana back safe and sound. And then he'd never touch the stuff again.

He plunged the needle into the vein on the inside of his elbow. The next moment a monster of a *toro* went charging through his blood, and he groaned out of a mixture of pleasure and relief.

Minutes later he was taking a hot shower, and feeling just great. Then, dried, he put on fresh clothes: a pair of black denims and a navy polo shirt. He rubbed some gel into his hair, then combed it so that you could see the tracks. He stepped into his leather slippers. He was being upbeat. He wanted to look presentable for when he was reunited with Ana later. As he told himself he was sure to be. There were going to be no hitches or glitches. No gremlins or hobgoblins. Everything was going to be just fine.

He had a shaky moment in front of the bathroom mirror, as he spread shaving foam over his face. What if things didn't go okay?

He found himself imagining what he would do if anything happened to Ana. Pictured himself waging a personal crusade against the Russians who'd taken her. He'd start by burning the *puticlub* down, then go after the Mr. Big personally. Get him on his own some place, and go to work on the bastard...

Velázquez realized that he was letting his imagination run away with him. He reminded himself of the importance of acting like a pro at all times. Even now, when the wires of his private and professional lives had crossed.

Especially now, he told himself, as he started in with the razor.

Stay upbeat and professional, and everything would be okay. If he'd ever had a code to live by then that was it.

Once he'd finished shaving, he went into the kitchen and fixed himself a strong mug of coffee with toast. He poured olive oil on the toast and ate it at the kitchen table. He wasn't hungry, but he forced himself to eat. He was going to need to be sharp and wide-awake for Ana today, and it was hard to be at your best on an empty stomach.

When he'd finished the toast, he went and sat on the sofa, next to the phone, and waited. Thoughts of Ana flooded his mind. He remembered a time early in their relationship when he'd been making love to her on the beach late at night, and they'd just slipped into a nice rhythm when some bastard showed up and nicked her handbag. Velázquez got up and went after the guy, and brought him down with a crashing rugby tackle before he retrieved the handbag; but Ana was annoyed when he handed it back to her. Confused, he asked her what was wrong. 'I was just about to come, you bastard!' she yelled. And then they'd both laughed their heads off.

That had been four years ago. But it felt like yesterday.

Velázquez realized that he was still as madly in love with Ana, as ever.

But this was all so unfair on her.

Ana didn't deserve to be kidnapped just because she was living with a cop.

If she'd been with another guy none of this would have happened to her.

Velázquez took all the blame on himself.

But no, it wasn't him that had taken Ana – it was the bastard Russian, whoever the son of the great whore was.

He told himself that wallowing in feelings of guilt never helped anyone – particularly if the guilt was misplaced.

He realized that his thoughts were becoming circular. That was supposed to be a sign you were depressed. But who wouldn't be depressed, if they were in his shoes right now?

And to think I was forever complaining about her decision to become a professional bullfighter, he thought. Who am I to tell a girl like Ana what she can or can't do?

The phone began to ring.

Velázquez's thoughts stopped in their tracks, and he picked up. '*Diga*?'

'*Hola*, Inspector Jefe. Have you got the CD-Rom?'

'Yes, but I want to speak to Ana before I hand it over.'

'She's okay, I promise you.'

'I want to hear that from her.'

'You're just going to have to trust me,' the Russian said. 'You take the CD-Rom to my people. They pick you up in a helicopter and bring it to me. You got that?'

'*Si.*'

'I look at the CD-Rom and check it is the one I need. Then if everything is in order, you get to leave with your wife.'

'Okay, but when do I get to see Ana?'

'All in good time, Inspector Jefe,' the man said. 'And remember – you come alone. We'll be watching you. So if there's anyone coming behind you, the deal's off and you can say goodbye to your wife forever.'

'There won't be anybody with me.'

'I hope not, for your wife's sake, because she seems nice. Contrary to what you might think, Inspector Jefe, I am not some crazy sadistic murderer. I am a businessman. I do only what is necessary for my business to thrive. I do not like to make nice young women disappear. I can do it – and I will do it, if I need to. But it doesn't need to come to that if you are sensible. Do we understand each other?'

'Yes.'

'Good, I am glad to hear that, Inspector Jefe.'

'So give me a time and a place.'

'Do you have a pen and paper handy?'

Chapter 21

Velázquez pulled up in a parking area several kilometres south of Utrera, and sat there and waited, wondering when the fuck the Russian was going to call. And hoping that Ana was all right.

But of course she is, he told himself. The Russian wouldn't have harmed her.

Why should he? What would he gain from that?

Nothing.

It was a matter of a simple exchange. I give the man what he wants, and he lets Ana go. End of story. No reason to worry about anything.

Velázquez was nervous as fuck even so. He'd had some nasty criminal bastards try to touch his balls or *cojones* in his time. It was something that was to be expected in his line of work. But what this Russian son of the great whore had pulled was a whole new category of ball touching.

Velázquez would like to get his hands on the man and tear him apart. But he had to try to stop thinking like that, and stay calm and professional for Ana's sake. Just then, he heard what sounded like the thunder of a helicopter. He looked out the window and saw what looked like a giant metallic insect in the distance. It was coming his way.

His mobile began to vibrate on his thigh and he snatched it up. '*Diga*?'

'Get out of your car, Inspector Jefe.'

'Then what?'

'Just get out.'

Velázquez did as he was told.

'Now look up.'

'I can see a helicopter.'

'It is about to land. Walk towards it.'

The line went dead, and Velázquez set off into the field in front of him. He could see that the helicopter was starting to come down, and the grass looked like it was getting a blow dry from some super-powerful hair dryer.

Velázquez began to run as the helicopter prepared to land. He saw two men climb out of the craft and come towards him. They were wearing tracksuits and Nike trainers, balaclavas and shades. They could be anyone.

The important thing he noticed about the two men was that they were both carrying guns. The taller of the two told Velázquez to hand over the CD-Rom.

'Where is Ana?' Velázquez yelled back. The noise from the helicopter was deafening.

'First the CD-Rom.'

'No, I want to see her. Where is she?'

'She is okay. Nothing happen to her. You do not need to worry. You give me CD-Rom and I take it to my boss. He is happy then he lets the girl go.'

Velázquez reached inside his leather jacket, and the shorter man jerked the hand in which he was holding his gun and shouted: 'Stop or I shoot!'

'The CD-Rom's in my pocket.'

'Wait.'

The taller one came over and frisked Velázquez, and he laid his hand on the CD-Rom while he was about it. He reached into the Inspector Jefe's pocket and helped himself to the article that all this fuss was about.

Velázquez's heart sank. He felt as though he had played this all wrong. He was handing over the CD-Rom in return for nothing.

He told himself he shouldn't be feeling this way. After all, had he not agreed to hand over the CD-Rom first, when he'd talked to Mr. Big on the telephone?

He'd had no alternative but to go along with what the man said.

Yet even so, he had a bad feeling about the way all this was going. Rage welled up inside him. 'Tell that boss of yours that if anything happens to Ana,' he yelled, 'I'll chase him down and kill him.'

'You will hear from my boss. He will call you. But you have to be patient. You are not in a position to make threats.'

The Russians made their way back to the helicopter and climbed aboard, then it took off. Velázquez felt like he was standing in a wind tunnel: his clothes were blown back against his body, and his hair was going every which way. He couldn't remember ever having felt so bad. I've made a right mess of this, he thought. I shouldn't have tried to do it alone. If Ana is killed after the way I've handled this…

He shat on the kidnappers' forebears as he made his way back to the car and climbed in behind the wheel. No sooner had he started the engine up than his mobile began to vibrate in his pocket. '*Diga*?'

'It's me, boss. Just wondering what's going on at your end?'

Velázquez said, 'I think I've probably acted like an idiot, José,' and told the Subinspector what had happened.

'Maybe you shouldn't've done it alone, boss.'

'That's the very last thing I want to hear right now, the way I'm feeling.'

'Sorry, I didn't mean to…' Gajardo broke off. 'Anyway, the Russian might keep his side of the bargain now and let Ana go.'

'But what if he doesn't?'

The two men listened to each other breathing down the line. Gajardo said, 'So now what?'

'I've just got to hope the Russian calls me back.'

'I've got the copies from Luz, boss.'

'Lock the CD-Roms in your desk and see if you can find out anything about the figurine in the blow-ups,' Velázquez said. 'We need to know who the sculptor is that made it, or who sold it…anything you can come up with.'

'I'll go round some of the galleries and antique shops in the city, and see what I can find out. Shall I get Serrano, Pérez and Merino on it, too?'

'Handle it yourself. I thought I told you to keep all this under your hat.'

'Sure, boss.'

'And be sure to let me know straightaway if you turn anything up.'

Velázquez hung up and tossed his mobile onto the vacant passenger seat, then started the engine up and set off for Seville.

He had just reached the outskirts of the city when his mobile began to ring. He snatched it up. '*Diga*?'

'It's not the right CD-Rom, Inspector Jefe.'

Velázquez swerved to miss a car, then slowed to a halt for a red light. His heart was busy doing somersaults. 'The fuck are you talking about?'

'The CD-Rom…you brought me the wrong one.'

'But it's the one that Fyodor's brother, Vassily, gave me.'

'Fyodor? Vassily? Who are these people?'

The motorist in the car behind was parping his horn. The light had changed. Velázquez set off again, steering with his right hand, jamming the phone to his ear with his left. Adrenaline raced through his veins like a wild bull. 'You know, the girl Lena's boyfriend.'

'Lena, yes, you took her. Where is she?'

'She didn't want to work for you.'

'She owes me money.'

'She seemed to think she'd paid you off.'

'Your attitude is most surprising, Inspector Jefe,' the Russian said. 'You are not talking like a man who loves his wife.'

'Let me talk to her.'

'The CD-Rom, Inspector. I need the right one.'

'It's the one that Ramón Ochoa took from Vladimir Vorosky.'

'Who told you that?'

'I can't tell you that, but I know that my source is honest.'

'There were two CD-Roms, Inspector Jefe, and you gave me the wrong one. That is all that concerns me. And it should be all that concerns you, if you want to see your wife again.'

Velázquez hit the brakes as a pedestrian stepped out into his path on a crossing.

'Look, I need to speak to my wife.'

The kidnapper had already hung up.

Tears streamed down Velázquez's cheeks as he headed along the Paseo de Cristobal Colon. He dried his face with the back of his hand, and told himself he'd really fucked up this time.

Now what? he wondered, as he crossed the bridge. He drove up Blas Infante, then turned into a side street and pulled over. He reached into his jacket pocket and brought out the baggie he'd brought with him, along with the hypodermic needle and other paraphernalia that were part and parcel of the junkie's kit; then he heated the heroin in the spoon, before he filled the syringe. And as he did these things, he realized that he had come to love every part of the ritual that led up to the moment he injected himself. He loved having to carry his addict's paraphernalia around with him, too. He loved taking it out and using each thing for its allotted purpose.

Or perhaps he meant for its wrong purpose.

But he also hated himself for loving all this the way he did.

Just as he jabbed the needle in, his mobile began to jive across the passenger seat. He waited a beat, then another, as the wild bull that was heroin careered through his veins. Then he snatched up his phone. 'José?'

'Have you talked to the Russian again yet, boss?'

'Just now,' Velázquez said, his mind reeling as the heroin did its work. He took a deep breath as he threw his head back on the rest, his eyes rolling.

He heard Gajardo say, 'Boss?' down the line.

Velázquez swallowed hard, then said, 'The man says there are two CD-Roms and I gave him the wrong one, so he's keeping Ana until I bring him the one he wants.'

'Mierda.'

'How's your search for the sculptor going?'

'That's the good news I was calling you about, boss,' Gajardo said. 'I've found out who the sculptor is, and I'm on my way to his studio on Calle Gerona right now.'

'What's the number?'

Gajardo told him.

'See you there in a few minutes.'

Velázquez saw Gajardo standing by his car up ahead. He parked with two wheels on the pavement, then jumped out and ran over to the door. The Subinspector pressed the buzzer to the studio, and a gruff masculine voice said, '*Hola*?'

Gajardo told the man who they were. 'We need to talk to the sculptor Antonio Ferrer.'

'That's me. What do you want to talk to me about?'

'If you come down, *señor*, then we can tell you.'

A couple of minutes later, the large wooden door creaked open. Velázquez and Gajardo found themselves looking at a big man with a bushy black beard, dressed in a pair of baggy old jeans and a stained black T-shirt that did nothing to hide his beer belly. Gajardo produced the blow-up he'd brought with him. 'We need to know if this figurine is your work?

Antonio Ferrer took the blow-up and looked at it. 'Yes, it is.'

'You are quite sure?'

'No question about it,' the sculptor said. 'I do recognize my own work.'

'How many copies did you run off?'

'None. I'm an artist, not a factory.'

'Who did you sell it to?'

'Jorge Villalba, the politician.'

Velázquez said, 'Do you know where he has the figurine?'

The sculptor shrugged. 'In his home, I presume.'

'Have you ever been there?'

'*Si*…once.'

And did he have the figurine there?'

The sculptor nodded.

Velázquez took out notebook and pen, saying, 'Where does the man live?'

Antonio Ferrer produced his mobile and pushed a few keys. 'Here it is,' he said, and read out the address. 'But what's all this about?'

'Nothing important, *señor*,' Gajardo said. 'Just routine.'

The sculptor's dark eyes narrowed. 'Doesn't sound like it to me.'

'Thanks for your help, Señor Ferrer.'

Velázquez turned to Gajardo, 'We'll take my car.'

Jorge Villalba's house was one of the beautiful old palaces on Calle San Vicente that were once the preserve of the Spanish aristocracy. Velázquez rang the buzzer but nobody answered. 'We need to get in there and take a look around,' he said.

'We'll need a warrant, boss.'

'No time for that.' Velázquez pushed the buzzer again. There was still no answer, so he tried the flat below. A man's voice asked who was there, and Velázquez introduced himself. 'We've come here to speak to Señora Villalba.'

The man buzzed them in, and they took the lift up to the top floor and rang the bell to the flat. Nobody came to the door, so Velázquez took out the lock picks he always carried with him and set to work. It didn't take him long to get the door open, and they entered the flat and started going through the spacious and elegantly furnished rooms one by one, on the lookout for the small figurine…and they found it sitting on the mantelpiece in the main living room.

They found something else there, too: a man lying on the sofa. There were bullet wounds to the head and chest. The man was taking the long *siesta* from which there's no return.

Gajardo said, 'Seems we got here too late, boss.'

Velázquez touched the victim's cheek. 'Not by long,' he said. 'The body's still warm.'

They checked the rest of the house, to make sure the killer wasn't hiding anywhere. But the place was empty.

'D'you reckon Villalba's one of the men on the CD-Rom, boss?'

'Got to be a good bet,' Velázquez said. 'Let's go and take another look at him.'

Gajardo followed the Inspector Jefe back into the living room. 'What are we looking for exactly?'

Velázquez undid the belt on the victim's trousers, then turned the body over and slid the trousers down. 'Now there's a coincidence, José.'

There was a large strawberry mark on the victim's right buttock.

'We've got our answer, boss. He was in the CD-Rom,' Gajardo said. 'They must've filmed it here. But who d'you reckon killed him?'

Velázquez shrugged. 'You know as much as I do.'

'Just wondered if you had a hunch?'

'I'm a police detective, José, not el puto Sherlock fucking Holmes.'

'Just as well, because I've never fancied playing the role of Doctor Watson.' Gajardo was looking around the room, in case the murderer had dropped the gun. 'No obvious sign of the murder weapon, boss.'

'We'd better search the flat for it properly, just in case.'

Velázquez was all but certain that they wouldn't find any gun, though, and he turned out to be right.

He took out his mobile and called the Jefatura. Then when the desk sergeant picked up, Velázquez identified himself and said, 'There's been a murder. I need you to get the Policía Científica team over here a.s.a.p.'

'What's the address?'

Velázquez told him, then hung up and said, 'I'm going to take a drive over to Jesús del Gran Poder to have another word with Father Antonio.' He suspected the priest had been holding out on him.

'Want me to go with you, boss?'

'No. I need you here for when the forensics and the fingerprint experts show,' Velázquez said. 'Call me if you manage to turn anything up, okay?'

Velázquez drove the short distance over to the Plaza de San Lorenzo. He pulled up outside the Iglesia de Jesús del Gran Poder, jumped out of the car and ran over the square, then went in through the Gothic archway and into the sacristy.

There was no sign of Father Antonio, or anyone else. Velázquez made for the priest's office. He had a hunch Father Antonio might have hidden the CD-Rom there. Where else would a priest keep something like that? It had to be there or in the man's flat.

Velázquez tried the door. It was locked. The Inspector Jefe took out his lock picks and went to work. He had the door open in next to no time. He rushed into the room and went over to the desk and rifled the drawers. No good. What about the bookcase? He got down on his haunches and started taking the Bibles and prayer books out. Concealed behind them was a CD-Rom. Velázquez felt sure it must be the one he needed.

He put it in his pocket, then hurried back out to his car, climbed in behind the wheel and set off for the Jefatura.

Chapter 22

Velázquez found Luz Cano working at her desk, and told her he had another favour to ask. He brought out the CD-Rom. 'This is a different one,' he said. 'I need you to do the same as you did with the other.'

'Make copies?'

Velázquez nodded. 'First I need to watch it, though. And I'll need you to make some blow-up stills, if the faces of the perpetrators are on the footage this time, okay?'

'Sure.' Luz took the CD-Rom and slid it into the laptop, then pushed *play*.

But this time nothing happened. She tried it again.

No go.

'What's up?' Velázquez asked her.

'It won't open. It must be encrypted.'

'Are you saying you can't play it without tapping in some secret code first?'

'That's right. I take it you don't know the code?'

Velázquez shook his head. 'Is there any way round this?'

'Only way's to break the code.'

'Which ain't gonna be easy, right?'

'It's a job for the experts.'

Velázquez had to work to get his thoughts and emotions under control. He shat on the forebears of the Russian who had taken Ana, whoever the bastard was. 'I'll need to have the best people working on it,' he said. 'If our people can't do it then get Spanish Intelligence involved – whatever it takes. And I need this done fast. It's an emergency and the clock's ticking. My wife's life is at stake.'

He made to leave, then stopped at the door and turned. 'Oh, and I'll need you to make two copies for me to take a.s.a.p., like you did with the other one. And run off others for whoever you get workin on it.'

'Okay,' Luz said, 'leave it with me.'

The Inspector Jefe drove back over to the crime scene, where Gajardo was watching the Policía Científica team go about their work. '*Hola*, boss,' the Subinspector said. 'Manage to turn anything up?'

Velázquez told him how he'd found the second CD-Rom but was unable to watch it because it was encrypted. 'What's been happening here?'

Gajardo shrugged. 'Nobody's telling me anything yet.'

'Still early days,' Velázquez said. 'I want you to come with me over to the Russians' *puticlub.*'

'What's the plan, boss?'

'I'm going to leave a message for the kidnappers.'

The club's dark and air-conditioned interior was a shock to the system after the heat and sunny brightness of the street. Over on the stage, a girl was busy trying to wrap herself around a metal pole. Her aerobic efforts were in marked contrast to those of her audience of middle-aged Spanish males, none of whom looked like they had done anything more athletic than lift a drink in the past few decades.

Velázquez squeezed in between a couple of the oldsters, and told the muscled barman he wanted to speak to his boss. The Russian squinted, wary as a fox, then said, 'He's not here. What do you want?'

'Tell him I've got his CD-Rom, and I'm willing to hand it over in exchange for my wife. You got that?'

The barman nodded. 'You'd better leave your number.'

'He's already got it.'

Velázquez turned and went back out, with Subinspector Gajardo in tow.

'Now what, boss?'

'We wait for him to call.'

'What if he doesn't?'

'Oh, he'll call all right,' Velázquez said. 'The CD-Rom is very important to him.'

Velázquez put the car in gear and set off. 'May as well go and see how they're progressing with the code while we're waiting, José.'

The breeze that swept in through the open windows was hot as a hair-dryer as they drove to the Jefatura. Velázquez left the Alfa Romeo in the basement car park, then he and Gajardo took the lift up and went in search of Luz Cano. They found her at her desk. 'I've got our guys and Spanish Intelligence working on it,' she said. 'No luck as yet, though, I'm afraid. They're doing everything they can, but it's a tricky one.'

Velázquez's mobile began to buzz in his pocket. '*Diga*?'

'*Hola*, Inspector Jefe. I hear you have something for me?'

'I've got the CD-Rom.'

'You are sure it is the right one this time?'

'Yes.'

'How did you come by it?'

'How did you kidnap Ana?'

'Do you always answer a question with another question?'

'Only when my wife's been kidnapped.'

'I see you have not lost your sense of humour, Inspector Jefe,' the Russian said. 'We took her in an ambulance – but you already know this. Now tell me: have you watched the CD-Rom?'

'No.' Velázquez was confused. 'But there's no way you could've known Ana was going to get gored during the *corrida*.'

'We took the precaution of drugging her beforehand. That way she was bound to lose consciousness before too much time had passed. And we had our men and the ambulance on standby, ready to take her when she did.'

'She was badly gored. For all I know you could be lying,' Velázquez said, 'and she could be dead, you son of the great whore!'

'Bullfighting is a very risky business, Inspector Jefe, it's true. But in this instance your wife was not gored.'

'That's a lie. I saw the blood myself.'

'Not hers.'

'Huh?'

'Our people had a bag of blood on hand, so as to make it look as though she'd been gored. Just a matter of having our man pour it over her tunic.'

'But how did you drug her?'

'There was something put in the energy drink she always has in the dressing room before a bullfight,' the Russian said. 'You see, we are professionals and do our homework, Inspector Jefe.'

'But she could've been killed if she'd been groggy or passed out when the bull charged!'

'We doped the bull a little beforehand – not enough to make it too obvious, but just enough to slow it down and make it a little less aggressive. And we had a marksman at the bullring who would've been able to shoot the bull with a tranquilizer if it had been necessary. We also had a surgeon at hand, in the unlikely event there was an accident. The risk of something bad happening to your wife was minimal, I assure you. And now I must tell you that I am getting tired of all your questions, and I need you to answer mine. Tell me, how can you be sure it's the right CD-Rom?'

'This one's encrypted.'

'I see…in that case, I would like to see it.'

'Listen,' Velázquez said. 'This time we're going to do things differently. I'm only prepared to make a direct exchange: the CD-Rom for Ana.'

'For all I know this could be a trick.'

'This CD-Rom is from the same person. The only difference is that this one is encrypted. I suspect that you can see the faces of the men on this one. And I'm assuming that's why you want it?'

'So you watched the other one, Inspector Jefe?'

'I'm afraid I did. It made me want to throw up.'

'Yes, there are some sick people out there.'

'Anyway, I'd say we have business to do.'

'Indeed.'

'This time we meet face to face. You bring my wife to me, and I give you the CD-Rom.'

'I will need to take the CD-Rom away with me first, to check it is the one I want. Then if it is, I will release your wife later the same day.'

'No, it's got to be a straight swap. I give you the CD-Rom and Ana leaves with me. If you don't bring her with you then I don't hand over the CD-Rom.'

'But how will I know it's the right one? You could even try to trick me and give me a CD-Rom with nothing on it.'

'So bring a laptop and check it when we meet.'

The line went quiet while the Russian gave the matter some consideration. Finally he said, 'You make a lot of demands for somebody in your position.'

'I disagree.'

'You talk tough, but I don't think you quite realize who you are dealing with.'

'I can play tough, too. Up until now I've been playing by the rules, but if anything happens to Ana then the rulebook goes out of the window.'

'What do you mean by that?'

'Take that club of yours…something nasty could happen to it.'

'Such as?'

'I don't know…a fire, perhaps.'

'I hope you are not trying to threaten me, Inspector Jefe?'

'I'm simply telling you the way it is,' Velázquez said.

'You have a way of talking more like a criminal than a police detective.'

'I'm talking like a man who is prepared to do whatever it takes to get his wife back.'

They both went quiet for a moment, then Velázquez said, 'Anyway, this is a simple matter. There's no need to complicate things. You want the CD-Rom. And I have it. So you bring your laptop and my wife to the place where we arrange to meet. I'm sure you know the code to open the CD-Rom.'

'What makes you so certain of that?'

'The way I have it figured, you must've had one of your men plant the camera in the room at Villalba's place beforehand,' Velázquez said. 'It must've been one of these tiny spy cameras that are easy to conceal. Am I right?'

'Go on.'

'So as I was saying, you can check the CD-Rom in the café where we arrange to meet. And then, once you've satisfied yourself that it's the right one, as I'm sure you will, I get to leave with my wife. That way we both win.'

'Okay, have it your way, Inspector Jefe. But you must allow me to decide where to meet, and you must come alone.'

'No. I'll be bringing my number two with me, and you bring one of your men. Only bring the one, otherwise it's no deal.'

They both went quiet, and Velázquez listened to the Russian breathing down the line.

'Okay, Inspector Jefe,' the man finally broke the silence. 'You bring your partner with you, but I decide the time and place. I'll call you again shortly.'

The line went dead.

Velázquez reached into his jacket pocket, and brought out his baggie. There was enough for another hit.

Maybe two, if he rationed himself.

Chapter 23

Just over an hour later, Velázquez was waiting outside of a café on Calle Juan de Mariano. It was a nondescript little affair. Hardly the sort of place where you'd ever expect anything exciting to happen.

Velázquez was nervous and fidgety. He kept looking at his watch.

A top-of-the-range BMW pulled up, and Velázquez's pulse switched to taurine mode. He exchanged glances with Gajardo.

Two men climbed out of the BMW. One was tall and of medium build, dressed in a smart grey suit and carrying a laptop. The second man was stocky, wearing jeans, Nikes and black sports jacket. They came over to Velázquez and Gajardo, and stopped just in front of them on the pavement. 'Nice day for it,' said the one in grey.

'Usually is in Seville,' the Inspector Jefe said. 'But I thought it was only the English who like to talk about the weather.'

'I've always been a big admirer of the English.'

'You won't find many of them here, except for the odd language teacher.'

The Russian's face creased in a forced smile. 'To business, then. If you'd like to give me the CD-Rom.' He held out his hand, in the expectation of receiving the object he clearly treasured.

'Where's Ana?'

'She's in the car.'

'Get her out here.'

'First I need to see the CD-Rom.'

'No, either you bring her out here now or the deal's off.'

The Russian looked at Velázquez and didn't say anything.

'You can leave your friend here outside the café with Ana and Subinspector Gajardo,' the Inspector Jefe said. 'You and I can go into the café and conduct our business at a table in there. You check the CD-Rom out. Once you've satisfied yourself it's the one you want, you take the CD-Rom and leave with your friend and Ana stays with us. That way everyone's happy. It's what we agreed.'

The Russian kept staring at Velázquez. Velázquez stared back at him.

Seconds passed.

Finally the Russian said, 'And what are you gonna do if I say no?'

'I've already told you that.'

'I'd like to hear you tell me to my face.'

'I'd get to keep the CD-Rom.'

'And if something should happen to your beloved wife, Inspector?'

'That wouldn't be wise of you.'

'Accidents happen.' The Russian produced his nasty smile. 'I speak hypothetically, of course.'

'Speaking hypothetically,' Velázquez said, 'if something of the sort you just mentioned were to happen, then I'd do whatever it would take to bring you down. Whether it's inside or outside of the law.'

'I could have you shot, if you want to play it like that. Don't think that wouldn't be easy.'

'I'll take my chances.' Velázquez shrugged. 'But what you just said cuts both ways.'

The Russian grinned. 'I see your talents are wasted working as you do as a policeman, Inspector.' He nodded to the bodyguard he'd brought with him, and the man went over to the car.

Velázquez watched him open the door and help Ana out. She looked over at Velázquez. If she was scared then she certainly didn't show it. That woman hasn't half got some *cojones*, Velázquez thought. His pulse raced as he watched the man take Ana by the arm and bring her over to the pavement.

Velázquez smiled at her. 'Are you all right, Ana?'

She nodded.

'Okay, Inspector Jefe,' said the Russian, 'how about we go and see to our little business matter?'

'After you.'

Velázquez followed the Russian into the café. The place had a tiled floor, and there were pictures of bullfight scenes and *toreros* on the whitewashed walls. A propeller fan hung from the ceiling, sending out intermittent waves of hot air, and the murmur of conversation trailed across the room from the men who were lined up at the counter, some of them standing and others sitting on stools.

Velázquez and the Russian went over to one of the vacant tables next to the window. The man pointed and said, 'You sit this side.'

Velázquez waited for the man, watching him carefully, and sat down at the same time as he did.

The Russian said, 'Put your hands on the table, where I can see them,' then he took out his laptop and booted it up.

Moments later, the man looked at Velázquez and said, 'The CD-Rom, Inspector Jefe.'

Velázquez took out one of the two copies he'd picked up from Luz earlier and handed it over.

A young waitress came over and asked what she could get them. Velázquez ordered two coffees, just to get rid of her.

The waitress smiled and went away.

Meanwhile, the Russian had fed the CD-Rom into the laptop, and was now busily tapping away at the keys.

Velázquez figured the man didn't want him to see what was on it. He'd be able to see for himself, anyway, just as soon as the experts had cracked the code – assuming they were able to do so.

The waitress returned with the coffees, then she went away again.

The Russian had stopped tapping at the keys by now. He must have got the CD-Rom open, Velázquez thought. And said, 'It's the right one this time, isn't it?'

'One moment, Inspector Jefe. I would like to see a little more.'

Velázquez glanced at his watch. The second hand was dragging like a bastard. He looked through the window and saw Gajardo and Ana standing out there, along with the Russian's bodyguard. Rivers of sweat were coursing down Velázquez's back.

The Russian turned the computer off, then closed the lid. 'This time you have delivered the right CD-Rom, Inspector Jefe,' he said. 'Congratulations on an excellent piece of work. Now you are free to take your wife.'

Seeing the Russian reach into his pocket, Velázquez reached into his jacket for his gun. 'There's no need to be nervous, Inspector. I am just going to take out some money to pay for the coffees,' the Russian said. 'We don't want to walk out without paying and have the girl call the police, now do we?'

Velázquez held the handle of his gun, ready to draw as he watched the man. The Russian brought his hand up out of his pocket. He held it out, palm upwards. There were some coins on it. He dropped them onto the table. 'You should know that my bodyguard is armed,' he said. 'I have instructed him to kill your wife first, if you try anything on the way out.'

The Russian got to his feet. Velázquez did likewise. He took out his gun and pointed it at the Russian's back as he followed the man out of the café.

Seeing that Velázquez was holding a gun, the bodyguard drew his weapon.

Velázquez moved in front of Ana. Then he said to the Russian and his bodyguard, 'There's no need for anyone to get hurt here.'

Mr. Big didn't even turn to look back as he made his way over to the BMW. His bodyguard went after him, walking backwards and keeping his gun pointed at Velázquez as he did so.

Velázquez kept his gun up, as he watched the pair climb into the car. He watched them pull out and then drive off, without a shot being fired.

The next moment Ana was in his arms. 'Oh, Luis,' she sighed, 'I knew I could count on you.'

'I've been frantic, Ana. Did those bastards hurt you in any way?'

'No, they treated me okay.'

Velázquez said a silent prayer of thanks.

Now that he had Ana back safe and sound, Velázquez recalled that he'd meant to talk to Lucia Segura again and drove over to the woman's flat. 'I'm afraid I'm busy,' she answered on the intercom after he had identified himself.

'I promise not to take up much of your time. This is important.'

She buzzed him in, and Velázquez took the lift up to the third floor. He rang the bell and heard slippered feet scuffing over the tiles, then the door opened. As before, Lucia Segura's slim form was clothed in tight black leggings and a top, and she'd caked her face in make-up. Her big dark eyes flashed him a look of sullen unwelcome from behind her long black tarantula lashes. 'I suppose you'd better come in,' she said, then took a step back to allow him to enter.

Velázquez was hit by the scent of jasmine as he passed through the door. He went and stood before a black-and-white photograph of Calle Betis by night. 'Take a seat, Inspector Jefe,' Lucia Segura said. Velázquez parked himself on the Laura Ashley sofa.

Lucia Segura reached down and took her Marlboros from the walnut coffee table. She helped herself to one and then offered Velázquez the pack. 'No thanks.' He shook his head. 'I quit five years ago.'

She shrugged. 'We've all got to die sooner or later.'
'Hopefully later.' Velázquez smiled.

She gave him a straight look then lit the cigarette, before she put the lighter back down on the coffee table. She found a small glass ashtray, and went and sat in one of the easy chairs. 'So what is it now, Inspector Jefe?'

'Your manuscript makes for fascinating reading,' he began. 'I wonder if I could talk to you about it some more?'

'Fire away.' She took a long drag on her Marlboro and deposited a few imaginary flakes of ash into the tray, which was balanced on her lap.

'The part that tells Father Pedro's account of his past was of particular interest to me. Father Pedro wrote that section himself, I believe, didn't he?'

'What I'd like to know is why you're making such a big deal about this, Inspector Jefe?'

'I'm working on a murder case, Señora Segura. Six men have been murdered. Two of them were priests, one of whom was Father Pedro Mora, as I believe you already know.'

'But I really don't see what any of that has to do with me and my little book.' She took another long drag, and peered at Velázquez through a cloud of smoke. 'Nothing that appears between the pages of my novel's going to bring him or any of the others back.'

'So it's a novel, then?'

'*Si, claro.*'

'Meaning that it's not fact, or what?'

'Did I say it was?'

'Well, novels are fiction, right?'

'*Correcto.*'

'Look, Señora Segura, I need you to tell me clearly and honestly whether Father Pedro's account, as it appears in your manuscript, was written by him or by you. Or did you make it all up?'

Lucia Segura's eyes flashed like warning signals through a pea souper. She thrashed her cigarette to death in the ashtray on her lap. 'Okay,' she said, 'if it's so damned important then you may as well know. I lied to you. It's all fiction. Every last bit of it. There. Are you happy now?'

'Including all of Father Pedro's account?'

'I said all of it, didn't I? Which one of those three short words was too long for you?'

'So do you mean to say Father Pedro never killed General Balmes?'

'I said it was fiction, Inspector Jefe. There, I made it easier for you. That's only one word.'

'But why didn't you tell us that earlier, *señora*?'

'I've no pension to speak of, and I've got to put some bread on the table the same as the next person.'

'You mean to say that you only think your book will stand a chance of selling if people believe it's true history?'

Lucia Segura appeared to shrug off her bitter attitude, the way a weary traveller drops her rucksack. 'Look,' she said, 'I'm sorry if I've wasted your time. The truth is, I feel rather ashamed of myself all of a sudden. I don't suppose it's much of an excuse, but I've got money worries and I thought the book might be a way of getting myself out of a hole if only I could get it published.'

If the woman wants to hear me tell her not to worry about it, she's gonna have a long wait, Velázquez thought. He got up and made for the door.

'Before you go, Inspector Jefe, there is one more thing that might be of interest to you.'

'I'm listening.'

'I was never romantically involved with Father Pedro Mora, but I did know him. He's from Burgat originally, the village I'm from, and...well, there were rumours about him.'

'Go on.'

'Like I said, it was just a rumour –'

'Tell me about it.'

'There was talk that he'd abused a boy.'

'In Burgat?'

She nodded. 'I don't know if you know the village?'

'I've never been there, but I've heard of it. It's not too far from Ronda.'

'That's right, about halfway between Ronda and the Costa del Sol. It's a tiny place, but most of the people who lived there back then have moved out by now. They had to in most cases, to find work.'

'What about Father Aloysius – was there a rumour about him, too?'

'No, he didn't live in Burgat.'

'When would this have been?'

'Back in the seventies, a year or two after General Franco died. I remember because I left the village in seventy-eight.'

'What was the name of the lad who was abused?'

'I never did find that out. Like I say, it was just a rumour, and it was a long time ago.'

'If you can try to think back and remember any more about it, then I'd very much like to hear about it.' Velázquez reached into his jacket and brought out his card. 'You can reach me on this number.'

Lucia Segura took the card and looked at it, and Velázquez went out.

Chapter 24

Burgat turned out to be little more than a bunch of whitewashed houses in a small valley, with a church positioned somewhere around the dip in the middle. The village was situated in the midst of a range of hills and mountains, roughly halfway between Ronda and the coast. The countryside was surprisingly green in places.

Velázquez pulled into a dusty little parking area at the edge of the village, and he and Gajardo climbed out. The sun was doing its worst, and Velázquez could feel the sweat running down his back. 'I'll take the first house,' he said, 'and you take next door, Jose.'

They had worked their way down to the bottom of the hill before either of them came across anyone who'd been in the village for more than twenty-five years. Many of the properties appeared to be shut up, and they learned from residents that several were holiday homes.

Then they knocked on the door of a woman who told them her father had lived in the village all of his life. Velázquez asked if he might have a word with him, and the Inspector Jefe was duly shown into the small living room where a man in his seventies was sitting in front of a television set. An old black and white Spanish film was showing. The woman told her father he had a visitor and invited Velázquez to take a seat. First Velázquez took out his ID and held it up for the man to see.

The man leaned forward to study it. Velázquez told the man that he was Inspector Jefe del Grupo de Homicidios in Seville, and that he was investigating the murders that had recently shocked the Andalusian capital.

The woman looked puzzled. 'So what are you doing in Burgat?'

'One of the victims was an old man who I have reason to believe lived in this village a long time ago – a Father Pedro Mora.'

177

'Yes, that's right,' the man said. 'I remember him. I read about what happened to him in the newspaper.'

'What was he like when you knew him?'

The man shrugged. 'I never knew him very well, to be honest.'

'But I should've thought everyone would have known each other in a small village like this in those days?'

'Yes, but I always kept my distance where he was concerned.'

'You mean you didn't like him or you aren't religious?'

'No, I'm not a believer, it's true...only it wasn't just that exactly.'

'What, then?'

'He always seemed to have the bad milk. And besides, there were rumours about him.'

'Rumours?'

'Yes...it was said he had tried to abuse a young boy in the village.'

'Did the police get involved?'

The old man shook his head. 'As far as I recall there were no witnesses. Nothing was proven, you know...although nothing very bad actually happened as it turned out, because the boy kicked him on the shin and managed to run away...So as I was saying, I kept my distance after I heard that.'

'When would this have been?'

'Oh, back in the seventies sometime. Not all that long after General Franco died.'

'Exactly how long after Franco's death?'

'A year or two, maybe.'

'What happened to the boy?'

'His family moved away. Of course he would be a grown man now. Javier Moreno Fafian his name was. Went for a sailor he did, Javi, I later learned. His mother used to write to us every year, you see. But then the letters dried up and we learned that she'd passed away. Cancer.'

'Any idea how I might find this Javier Moreno Fafian?'

'On a navy vessel, I should imagine.'

Once he was back in the street, the Inspector Jefe called Agente Pérez. '*Hola*, Sara, Velázquez here.'

'*Hola*, boss.'

'Have you turned anything up yet?'

'Afraid not.'

'In that case, can you get onto the Admiralty and find out where a Javier Moreno Fafían is right now. He's originally from Burgat.'

'Okay, I'll get on it.'

'It's important, so call me back as soon as you have something.'

'Will do, boss.'

They hung up and Velázquez went back to knocking on doors.

Just over an hour later, Agente Pérez called back. 'I've tracked Javier Moreno Fafían down for you, boss,' she said. 'He's on a ship that pulled into port down in Rota yesterday.'

'Got the name of the ship?'

'It's El Principe.'

'In that case, get yourself over to Rota and talk to him on the double.'

'I'm already on my way, boss.'

'Good work, Sara.'

They hung up

Subinspector Gajardo emerged from the door of the next house at that moment, just in time to see Velázquez aim a punch at the sky. 'Got a result, boss?'

'Very possibly, José,' Velázquez said. 'Pérez's on her way to talk to a man who might have been abused by Father Pedro Mora as a boy, back in the late seventies.'

Heroin was buzzing in Velázquez's veins as they headed back to Seville. He'd used the last of what was in the baggie he'd been carrying around with him, shooting up in the toilet of the only bar in Burgat before they left. His mobile began to ring, and he fished it out of his pocket. '*Hola*?'

'Luis, it's Luz. Good news – they've managed to decode the encryption.'

'You mean you've been able to watch the CD-Rom?'

'I sure have, and it's what you thought it would be like,' Luz said. 'Just like the other one, only this time you can see the faces.'

'Did you recognize any of the men on it?'

'Those two young gay guys that were shot in bed. I remember their faces from the photographs in the newspapers.'

'Who else?'

'That politician guy...what's-his-name – Villalba.'

'He's dead too. Who else?'

'And then there's the Mayor's lawyer, Alfonso Cayetano-Fitzmorgan. I know him because my friend was dating his son for a while.'

'He's still alive,' Velázquez said, thinking aloud. 'At least, he is so far as I know.'

'You think he could be next on the killer's hit list, right?'

'I'd bet my salary on it.'

'In that case, I suppose you'll be wanting to know where he lives,' Luz said.

'Do you mean to say you have an address?'

'I thought you might need it, so I did a little research to save you time.'

'You're a gem, Luz. Did anyone ever tell you that?'

Luz said, 'The man's got a big place over on Calle Bailen in the Old Quarter.'

'Know the number?'

Luz told him.

'We're on our way over there to talk to him now.'

Velázquez hung up and dropped his mobile onto his lap, then he put his foot down. And they had just reached the outskirts of Seville, minutes later, when his phone began to ring again. '*Hola*?'

'It's Pérez, boss.'

'Have you found Javier Moreno Fafían yet, Sara?'

'I've just been talking to the man.'

'And?'

'He said Father Pedro Mora tried to abuse him when he was eleven, but he managed to get away from him. He told his family what happened, and his father went to the police. Apparently officers in Ronda spoke to Father Pedro, but he denied it all and that was as far as the investigation went.'

'How long was Moreno Fafían away at sea?'

'He just got back from a three-month return trip to Argentina only yesterday…which means he obviously couldn't've killed Fathers Pedro or Aloysius.'

'No, but he could've got somebody else to do it for him.'

'I suppose it's possible…although I must say he didn't seem the type.'

'Killers rarely do.'

'Oh yes, I almost forgot,' Pérez said. 'One curious thing that I turned up – Javier Moreno Fafían happens to be the brother of Father Antonio, the priest who serves at the Iglesia de Jesús del Gran Poder. Apparently the priest had his surname changed to Dominguez Castillo some years ago.'

'My God, it's all fitting into place now.'

'What is, boss?'

'No time to explain, Sara. I'll fill you in on the details later.' Velázquez hung up and put his foot down.

Alfonso Cayetano-Fitzmorgan's place was an old five-storey palace of the sort that had once been the preserve of the city's aristocratic elite.

There was no response at the buzzer, so Velázquez picked the lock to get the front door open. They heard the murmur of voices and followed it to the study, where they found Alfonso Cayetano-Fitzmorgan and Father Antonio Dominguez Castillo.

The priest was holding a gun, and he had it pointed at the lawyer. '*Hola*, Inspector Jefe,' he said. 'I wondered when you were going to catch up with me.'

'Put the gun down, Father Antonio.'

'I can't do that, I'm afraid...you see, this man is an abuser of children.'

'I know all about that.'

'How did you find out?'

'I know about the CD-Rom,' Velázquez said. 'Not the one you gave me, but the one where you get to see the men's faces. And everyone who was on the film has already been murdered, with the exception of this man and the boy who was being raped.'

'This man is sick. He needs to die.'

'Come on, Father, priests aren't meant to kill people. You know that.'

'You think I'm crazy, is that it?'

Velázquez didn't say anything.

'Of course you do,' said Father Antonio. 'Many people would have it that religious faith itself is nothing more than a form of structured mass insanity, anyway. What is prayer, after all, they argue, but talking to someone who isn't there? Well, I'm here to tell you that the atheists are wrong, Inspector Jefe. God does exist, and he needs people to carry out his work here on Earth, as you policemen are clearly incapable of doing it.'

'Father Antonio,' Velázquez said, 'why don't you put the gun down and we can talk about all this at our leisure?'

'You'd like that, wouldn't you? You'd like me to let this servant of Satan off, so that he'll be free to do more evil, is that it?'

'I'd like him to have a fair trial, and then to be sent to prison for a very long time for his crimes.'

'His lawyer would probably get him off, Inspector Jefe. And even if he did get put away, he'd probably be out within a few years if he kept his nose clean.'

'Listen, Father Antonio, I know the system isn't perfect but it's the best hope we have of creating a decent and civilized society. Murder is wrong, Father. That's another thing I know. And if you think God wants you to kill this man, if He is up there looking down on this little scene, then I think you're wrong.

'And anyway, what about the idea of redemption? Doesn't it say in the Bible that every man should be given the opportunity to redeem himself?'

'Yes, but it also stresses the need to stamp out Satan.'

'Strikes me that you're trying to play God, Father Antonio.'

'You're wrong. I don't fool myself by thinking there's anything divine about myself. I'm just a man who is doing his best to carry out God's wishes.'

'If you ask me, it sounds like an awfully fine line you're treading.'

'Nobody ever said following God's wishes is easy, Inspector,' the priest said. 'Straight is the gate and narrow is the way.'

'Why don't you tell me about the other men on the CD-Rom, Father Antonio? Did you kill them, too?'

'God wanted it so. They were servants of Satan.'

'What about Fathers Pedro and Aloysius?'

'They were the same. They deserved to die.'

'One thing that confuses me, Father – why did you change your modus operandi after killing the two priests?'

'I wanted to give you the impression that there was more than one killer out there, Inspector Jefe.'

'And from what I've seen, I wonder if you hated the priests just that little bit more than your other victims? Is that why you killed them the way you did?' Velázquez exchanged glances with Gajardo, and then, before Father Antonio could reply, the two officers lunged at him.

Alfonso Cayetano-Fitzmorgan dived onto the floor and the priest fired the gun. The bullet got Alfonso Cayetano-Fitzmorgan in the leg, and he cried out.

The next moment, Velázquez was wrestling Father Antonio for the gun. Gajardo came at the priest from behind, then the two detectives wrestled him to the floor, and the Inspector Jefe was able to disarm him.

Velázquez took out his mobile and called for an ambulance, while Gajardo put a pair of plastic restraints on Father Antonio's wrists.

Chapter 25

That evening, Velázquez and Ana were sitting on stools with Gajardo at the long wooden counter in the Bar Eslava, drinking red wine and eating tapas. The place was packed to the seams, and people were jammed in at their back, so that the waiters had to keep handing dishes over and between them.

Velázquez was feeling good about things in general, now that he had Ana back safe and sound. Ana was a marvellous woman, and maybe he wasn't such a bad guy himself. What's more, Seville was a damn fine city, and the Bar Eslava was a hell of a good place to be in. Especially if you were eating the excellent food they served here, and washing it down with what was a pretty decent Rioja. The Inspector Jefe had passed a difficult moment or two a little earlier, but then he took a shot of methadone and now he was feeling as strong as a bull. The world really was, it seemed, a good place to be in. Or at least it could be, so long as you got your share of luck.

'So, what set Father Antonio on his killing spree?' Ana asked.

Velázquez picked up the wine bottle and replenished their glasses. 'You tell it, José,' he said.

Gajardo sipped his wine. 'The man was raped repeatedly by a priest at the orphanage as a boy.'

'Bit odd that he should've decided to enter the priesthood himself in that case, isn't it?'

'The way he saw it, his abuser, Father Miguel, served Satan, and Father Antonio wanted to serve God – '

'And for him,' Velázquez cut in, 'that meant killing all the bad priests.'

'The paedophile priests he knew of, you mean?' 'Exactly.'

Ana looked puzzled. 'I still don't get what led you to him, though.'

'It all really started to fall into place when we discovered Father Pedro Mora had tried to rape a boy by the name of Javier

Moreno Fafían, back in the seventies.' Velázquez sipped his wine. 'And then we found out that this Javier Moreno Fafían's actually Father Antonio's brother, only Father Antonio changed his surname from Moreno Fafían to Dominguez Castillo a few years back.'

'Then we found the priest at Alfonso Cayetano-Fitzmorgan's house when he got there,' Gajardo said.

'But what made you think of going there in the first place?'

'We wanted to talk to him.'

'Who, Alfonso Cayetano or Father Antonio?'

'Both of them…that is, we went there to talk to Cayetano, but the priest just happened to be there already.'

'And he was about to kill Cayetano?'

'We got there just in time,' Velázquez said.

'But I still don't get what Cayetano had to do with it all. Is he a paedophile, too?'

'That's right.'

'But what was it that put you onto him?'

Velázquez popped a piece of cod into his mouth, chewed and swallowed. 'He was one of the men on the CD-Rom.'

'What CD-Rom?'

'The one containing footage of a young boy being repeatedly raped.'

'I see.' Ana's brow furrowed as she took it all in. 'Why did the Russians who kidnapped me want a CD-Rom with some paedophiles on it so badly?'

'To use it to blackmail Cayetano,' Velázquez said. 'The man's a big cheese at the Town Hall.'

'Or was.' Gajardo grinned. 'Where he's headed, he's going to end up being someone's breakfast if he isn't careful.'

'Meaning you've got enough proof to put him away?'

'He's made a full confession.'

'Case solved, then.' Ana popped a piece of squid into her mouth and chewed. 'Sounds like you two have had a rather successful day.'

'You can say that again.' Velázquez reached for the bottle and gave himself a refill. He was about to replenish Gajardo's glass, too, when the Subinspector said he had better be leaving. There was somewhere he had to be.

'Enjoy the rest of your evening, José,' Ana said.

'Thanks…you two, as well.' He reached for his wallet. 'How much do I owe for the food and wine?'

'It's on me,' Velázquez said.

When Gajardo had left, Velázquez turned to Ana and smiled. 'I feel so bad about what happened to you,' he said.

'There's no need to feel like that, Luis. It wasn't your fault.'

'I'm not so sure about that. I mean, the Russian only kidnapped you to get at me.'

'That's true, I suppose. But I always knew you'd come and get me.' She chewed on a juicy chunk of cod before swallowing it. 'I know the kind of man you are.'

'What kind of man's that?'

She grinned. 'The sort that always takes the bull by the horns when the chips are down.'

Velázquez felt Ana's hand working up his thigh, and he thought how gorgeous she looked. 'Do you make a habit of that, Ana?'

'What…feeling men up, you mean?'

Velázquez's mobile began to vibrate in his pocket. He took it out and said, 'No, mixing your metaphors.' Then accepted the call and said, '*Diga*?'

'Great work, Inspector Jefe.' It was Diego Blanco.

'News travels fast, I see.'

'Like I always say, a dog can't take a poop in the street in this city without I get to know about it.'

'So it seems.'

'You must be feeling pretty happy with yourself.'

'I guess so,' Velázquez said. 'Although I still haven't managed to discover the identities of Bill and the Black Lady, much less track them down.'

'Bill and who?'

'Couple of nutters who stole my car a while back.' Among other things, Velázquez thought.

'Prob'ly working for the Russians and wanted you off their case.'

'Seems like that's your answer to most things, Diego, right?'

'Only because it's the way things are,' the gangster said. 'Anyway, I just thought I'd call to congratulate you on an excellent piece of police work, Inspector Jefe. And I see that Alfonso Cayetano-Fitzmorgan's been charged, so the Russians won't be able to use the CD-Rom to blackmail him now his secret's out.'

'That's true. It's all worked out rather well.'

'Don't be fooled, though – this is one battle you've won, but the war with the Russians is still far from over, Luis. Any time you need my help to run them out of town, you only have to call.'

'I'll bear it in mind.'

'Be sure to stay in touch.'

'Don't worry, I will.'

They hung up.

Ana said, 'Who was that?'

'Oh, just someone calling to congratulate me on solving the case.'

Ana sipped her Rioja and smiled. 'It's so great to be free and back together again, Luis.'

Velázquez took her hand in his and gave it a tender squeeze.

'You're too right it is,' he said in a voice that was raspy with emotion. 'I don't know what I would've done without you, Ana.'

His mobile burst into life again, but this time Velázquez decided to ignore it and let it ring.

Ana said, 'Aren't you going to answer it? It might be something important.'

He reached into his breast pocket and took it out. '*Hola?*'

A female voice he didn't recognize said, 'Is that Inspector Jefe Velázquez?'

'Speaking.'

'We haven't met, Inspector, but I'm Carmen Segura. I hope you don't mind me calling you on your mobile like this, but I wanted to talk to you on behalf of my mother, Lucia. You interviewed her recently, she told me, concerning a murder case.'

'Yes, on two occasions to be exact.'

'She told me about it.'

'So what can I do for you, *señorita*?'

'My mother has passed away and…well, I thought you ought to know.'

'Oh, I'm terribly sorry. But when did it happen?'

'Only a couple of hours ago,' Carmen Segura said.

There's no hint of foul play, I hope?'

'Oh no, nothing like that, Inspector Jefe. I think she'd got herself very stressed ever since she started writing the book she was working on. She'd had a stroke, and then she had what I later learned was a massive heart attack just before the ambulance arrived.'

'I'm very sorry, *señorita*. Please allow me to pass on my condolences.'

'Thank you, Inspector, but I'm really calling because my mother seemed to be very troubled about something she said to you.'

'Oh…and what was that?'

'She clearly wanted to talk and make a confession of some sort right at the end, but she was rambling, so I didn't understand much. I did understand, though, that she wanted me to call and tell you that she'd written a letter that was addressed to you.'

'I see…what's in the letter?'

'I'm not totally sure…it was sealed, and I wouldn't open it for the world. But my mother did tell me that she'd lied to you, Inspector, and this seemed to be troubling her.'

'Did she give you any specific details?'

'No, she was rambling, like I said. All I know is it had something to do with Father Pedro Mora and a General Balmes. That's all I could make out.'

'I see…so perhaps you can send me the letter, then?'

'I can do better than that – if you'd like to come to the funeral tomorrow morning, I'll hand it to you in person.'

'That's most kind of you.'

'The funeral will take place at eleven a.m., at the cemetery in Seville.'

'Okay, I'll see you there, Señorita Segura. Thank you very much for the call. And please allow me to pass on my condolences once more to you and your family.'

'Thank you, Inspector. Until tomorrow, then.'

They hung up.

Ana shot Velázquez a puzzled look, and he brought her up to speed. Then he paid the bill.

It was just a short walk back to the flat on Calle Teodosio, and as soon as they got in Velázquez took Ana in his arms. 'You don't know how much I've…' He was lost for words.

'What's the matter, Inspector Jefe?' Ana said. 'Something about your behaviour gives me the impression you want to make a powder.'

'I want to make love to you,' he said.

'It's the same thing, no?' Ana was making a joke, because when a Spaniard says he wants to make a powder, he means he wants to fuck.

Velázquez grinned. 'How about we do it and find out?'

They tore each other's clothes off.

Epilogue

There were only four other people at the funeral the following morning, apart from Velázquez and the priest. They were an old lady who looked like she must be Lucia Segura's sister, two other younger women, and a man of around the same age as the women. Inspector Jefe didn't recognize any of them.

Velázquez eyed the two younger women furtively as the priest said the last rites, and wondered which of them was Carmen Segura – the one in the trouser suit, or the one in the long dress?

As soon as the service was concluded, the woman in the black trouser suit came over and introduced herself. 'I'm the woman that called you yesterday, Inspector Jefe,' she said. 'Thank you for coming.'

'It was the least I could do.'

'I've brought this for you, like I promised.' She reached inside her jacket, brought out a letter and handed it to Velázquez. 'As I told you yesterday, Inspector,' Carmen Segura said, 'Mother seemed to be most troubled by the fact that she'd lied to you about something to do with Father Pedro Mora and this General Balmes, so I suspect it's about that.'

Velázquez opened the letter. It had been typed on two sheets of A4 paper.

He began to read:

Dear Inspector Jefe Velázquez,

I find that my conscience is troubled on account of some of the things I told you, and so I find I really must finally set the record straight.

To begin with, it's true that I was courted by a young man on Tenerife in the summer of 1936, and the young man in question did, to the very best of my knowledge, assassinate General Balmes; only the man involved was not Pedro Mora – or Father Pedro – but somebody quite different.

I was very much in love with the young man in question at the time, although I don't think I realized just how deeply until much later, by which time everything had gone wrong: the egg

190

had been smashed, as it were, and by then there was no putting the pieces that made up the shell back together again, as there never is.

So I must apologize, Inspector Jefe, for having lied to you on two accounts: firstly, when I told you that the man in my manuscript was the young Father Pedro Mora; and then a second time, when I told you that I'd made everything in my manuscript up and that it was all fiction.

The parts that I told you had been written by Pedro Mora were in fact written by my first love. He had his son trace me somehow, and sent his account to me through the post. He was dying of cancer and very near the end at the time, and I rushed to the hospital and was at least able to spend a little time with him before he passed away.

He assured me that everything he wrote in the account he sent me was true. The events at Almendralejo, joining the Republicans and the maquis in the Pyrenees... And he further assured me that what I'd heard my father telling my mother that day, in the summer of 1936, was also true: he had indeed killed General Balmes, thereby kick-starting the Civil War.

I see no reason to create a lot of stress and bother for his children by telling you his name; it is sufficient, I think, for me simply to tell you what really happened, and this I have now done.

Well, there it is. I subsequently married another man who bore me two lovely daughters, before he died five years ago.

That's all there is to tell. I feel better now that I've finally told you the truth, and got the whole thing off my chest (even though you won't actually get to read this letter until after I have passed away). I hate lying and liars, you see, and have always done my best to be honest all my life.

You strike me as being a good man, Inspector Jefe, and that only made the thought of having lied to you play on my conscience all the more.

I wish you well from beyond the grave.

With best regards,

Lucia Segura

Printed in Great Britain
by Amazon